THE CONSTANTINOPLE DIARIES
MURDER
IN THE GARDEN OF
ENCHANTMENT
A MADAME THEODOSIA MYSTERY
USA TODAY
BESTSELLING AUTHOR
KATHRYN GAUCI

First published in 2024 by Ebony Publishing

ISBN: 978-0-6487144-8-4

"At dawn I heard the nightingale lament
The scent of the rose had intoxicated his soul
He had lost himself, he knew not where
Marvel at this poor nightingale with love."

From "The Nightingale's Lament"
by Mehmed Muhyiddin Üftâde(1490–1580)

CONTENTS

Phanar
Naval Arsenal
PERA
British Embassy
Telegraph Office
Petits Champs
Galata Serai
Municipality
Assembly Gardens
Top Hane
Landing Place
Admiralty
des Morts
Austrian Embassy
Russian Embassy
Port of War
Municipality
Swedish Embassy
Sultan Selim Mosque
Azab Kapu
Gul Jami Mosque
Tower of Galata
GALATA
Sultan Selim
Jubali Kapu
Imp. Ottoman Bank
mruk
Atab Kapu Bridge
Port of
Quarantine
Commerce
Un Kapani
Steamers for Kadi Keui and P
Muhammad II Mosque
Steamers for the Goldenhorn
Steamers for Skutari
Yeni Baghcheh
Bosporus Steamers
Suleimanieh
Egyptian Bazaar
Custom House
Mosque
Sultan Valideh
War Office
RAILWAY STATION
Maidan
Demir Kapu

A NOTE ON 1900S CONSTANTINOPLE

During the Ottoman era, Constantinople was the name used by foreigners, expats, and minorities such as Greeks, Armenians, Levantines, Europeans, and Russians, but the city was always referred to as Istanbul by Ottoman Turks. Although official Ottoman documents and government communications were in Ottoman Turkish, the lingua franca of the elite, the wealthy, educated, and merchant classes was French. As part of a cosmopolitan society, many families spoke several languages fluently, and conversed in their own language at home. Shop signs in the fashionable districts, such as Pera, were often in several languages – French, Greek, English, Russian, Ottoman Turkish, and maybe German, Italian, or Arabic. International newspapers and magazines were readily available and could be found in many languages too. Religion and superstition played an important role in people's lives during this period.

CHAPTER 1

Constantinople: June 1900

EACH NIGHT BEFORE she retired to bed, Theodosia sat at her elegant Biedermeier desk in her study, opened her leather diary, dipped the reed of her pen in the inkpot, and began her entry for the day. Illuminated by the soft lamplight, the wet ink glistened for a few seconds on the page until it dried a deep Prussian blue, pleasing to the eye on the ecru-coloured paper. In this hour of solitude, the diary became an extension of her mind as she poured forth her thoughts and feelings onto the pages with the skill of an accomplished calligrapher, marvelling at the way the letters formed sentences, and the sentences became paragraphs.

The diary was one of the last gifts from her husband, Alexander. Aware that he was suffering from a debilitating illness with only weeks to live, he commissioned it for her from an Armenian bookbinder in the Grand Bazaar, taking careful note to choose the most exquisite marbled paper to line the inside of the book. Then he purchased a supply of pens and various coloured inks from a noted calligrapher which she kept in a special calligrapher's box, and presented it to her, telling her that whenever she felt alone, he was beside her while she wrote. During one of their last conversations, he told her that she must record the life she lived while it was still possible – for their daughter – as he was acutely aware that the Ottoman Empire was in its dying days and that things would soon change.

At the time he gave her the diary, she thought it too beautiful to use; that she might accidentally drop specks of ink on it or misspell a word and make the page look ugly, but on the day after his burial, steeped in loneliness and despair, she took it out of the drawer and started writing, pouring forth her thoughts as if she was conversing with him. It became her lifeline, her connection to the man she loved more than life itself – the man who had given her a beautiful daughter, who spoilt her with fine jewels and the latest Parisian fashions. Thus, it was because of him that she started to write.

Her diary entry that night began like the others: *Last night I dreamt you were by my side...* when she heard a knock on her door. Her manservant, Abdul Agha, entered the room, one arm behind his back and the other holding a gold tray with a calling card and a large envelope.

'What is this, Abdul?'

'They were delivered this afternoon when you were out.'

Theodosia looked at the calling card, which was from a Greek friend, Katerina, and then picked up the envelope sealed with red wax with an Ottoman inscription that she instantly recognised as belonging to the family of Ömer Pasha. On breaking the seal, she slid out a cream-coloured card with an engraved gold border and saw it was a wedding invitation. At the top, inscribed in decorative Ottoman script framed by a border of delicate roses was the family name, while the invitation itself was in French, handwritten in the most exquisite calligraphy.

'Oh how wonderful,' she remarked with great delight. 'Ömer Pasha and his second wife Hafsa's youngest daughter, Behice, is to be married to Hamid Bey, son of Ferid Pasha, a military advisor to the sultan, and I have been invited. What a glorious marriage this will be. They are both such fine people and Hamid is as handsome as Behice is beautiful.'

Theodosia approved of the marriage although she barely knew Hamid. 'I must see my dressmaker in the Grand Rue as soon as possible. I simply have to have something wonderful to wear for such a momentous occasion.'

Abdul Agha bowed slightly. 'Will that be all, madame?'

'Thank you, Abdul. Ask Calliope to make an appointment with Madame Eleftheria in the morning. Oh, and please tell Maria to make a warm glass of milk with honey and put it on my bedside table. I will retire to bed soon.'

'As you wish. Goodnight.'

As soon as Abdul left the room, Theodosia went back to her diary and continued her entry for the day. There was nothing like a wedding to lift the spirits, and such an invitation coming from the crème de la crème of Ottoman society delighted her immensely. The pen picked up pace as she added to her entry – *My dearest Alexander, last night I dreamt you were by my side... Today, I have good news and I know that you will be happy for me. An important marriage will take place in the polis and I have been invited.*

Theodosia blotted her entry, wiped her pen with a fine piece of silk, and closed the diary. Before retiring for the night, she picked up Alexander's photograph, which took prime place along with the diary on her desk, and kissed it. 'Goodnight, my darling.'

In the morning, she rose early and as usual discussed what she would be wearing with her maid, Calliope. She then took her daily stroll through the garden before joining her daughter, fourteen-year-old Electra, in the breakfast room where their cook, Maria, was just finishing setting the table. Walking through the garden before breakfast was a ritual Theodosia always enjoyed. From her home in Teşvikiye, with its beautiful garden covered with arbours of clematis, roses, and jasmine, she had a grand view overlooking the red roof tops towards the Bosphorus and Seraglio Point, a promontory quarter separating the Golden Horn and the Sea of Marmara further south. On the other side of the Bosphorus Strait was Üsküdar on the Asian side, gateway to the East, dotted with fishing villages and beautifully designed yalis, the summer palaces of Constantinople's elite, their facades painted in a palette of pastels as soft as the spring blossoms that sent forth their fragrance in the summer breeze. At this time of year, the garden was bursting with flowers and the heady scent of jasmine and roses filled the air. From spring to the end of summer, she often sat outside to eat her meals, or simply to relax and read a book. Every day, she thanked God that Alexander had the foresight to hire a gardener and create this slice of heaven for them while he could. Every rose, every fruit tree, they had planted together, and now he was no longer here to enjoy it with her. A tear slid down her cheek which she hurriedly wiped away when she heard her daughter call out from the terrace.

'Mama, breakfast is ready.'

By the time she reached the house, her thoughts had turned to the wedding again.

Electra gave her mother a kiss on the cheek. 'Good morning, Mama, you are in a good mood today.'

'You will never guess what arrived yesterday?' Theodosia showed her the wedding invitation. 'Of course, my darling, you are invited too.' She pointed to Electra's name. 'What an honour. I have asked Calliope to make an appointment with Madame Eleftheria. She has just arrived back from Paris and will tell us what the fashionable French ladies are wearing this summer. Do you realise, this is the first wedding I've been to since your father died? How it will cheer me up. It's been such a gloomy winter.'

The sun streamed through the breakfast room as they dined on an array of delicious food made by the family cook. Like Theodosia and Alexander, Maria was Greek and only a few years older than Theodosia herself. She had been in their employ since her marriage and was hired because her previous employers had moved to another part of the empire and decided not to take her. It was they who asked Alexander and Theodosia if they might consider hiring her.

Maria was from a poor Greek background in a village somewhere near Bursa and had been placed into the service of a local pasha when she was fourteen. At first she was one of many lowly household servants, but the pasha's family soon noted her interest in all things culinary and moved her to the kitchen where she worked under the chief cook, Master Yusuf, an elderly man who had once worked for Sultan Abdulaziz but left after the sultan's dethronement. "Chief Cook", as Master Yusuf was addressed, was a highly temperamental man, and seemingly unhinged at times due to what some believed was the sudden death of his master, classified as a suicide but thought by others to have been a murder. He was not in the habit of tolerating anyone in his domain who shirked their duties and showed no talent. A fierce man with a bad temper if things went wrong, he ran the kitchen with military precision, but if someone excelled, he displayed extreme warmth and showered them with praise – although never so much as to make them big-headed. When Maria first came to the Vasileiou household, she regaled Theodosia for hours with tales of Chief Cook and his passionate outbursts, like the time he threatened to slit a cook's throat with a carving knife because he overcooked the vegetables, beseeching Allah to smite the man down, or conversely, when he burst into tears at the scent and taste of the perfect baklava.

'Well no one here will chase you around the kitchen table with a knife,' Theodosia told her. 'You will be quite safe.' Although she did often hear squeals of laughter when Maria recounted the same stories to Electra and took a rolling pin, pretending to be Chief Cook, and playfully chased her around the wooden table.

'And then what would he do?' Electra would ask. She never tired of Maria's stories and often drew pictures of Chief Cook, who she imagined as the wicked giant in a fairy story, wielding a large knife, with blood dripping from it. Alarmed at seeing the red painted knife, Maria stressed that he never actually killed anyone, and that really he was as soft as a kitten underneath his hard shell.

Theodosia spread a small amount of mulberry jam on her toast and drank her tea which was served from the samovar on the sideboard. 'The wedding will take place in three weeks' time,' she said. 'I must think of something beautiful for a wedding gift.'

'What about a pair of embroidered bath towels for the hammam?' Electra suggested. 'Or napkins. You can never have enough of those?'

'We will go to Au Bon Marché and some of the other department stores after we've been to see Madame Eleftheria. They always have wonderful sets of fine porcelain and crystal ware. I don't even know where the couple will live when they are married.'

After breakfast, Electra went to her room where she was having an hour's German lesson with Fraulein Meyer, a young German teacher from Berlin, whose father was an engineer working in the city developing the plans for the new Berlin to Baghdad railway. In the meantime, Theodosia went over the day's menu with Calliope and Maria and then prepared herself for an outing in Galata and the Grande Rue de Pera.

At ten o'clock exactly, Abdul Agha arrived at the front entrance of the house with the carriage driven by two white horses to take Theodosia and Electra the relatively short distance from Teşvikiye to the Grand Rue, the most fashionable street in Constantinople. At this time of day, it was filled with pedestrians and other horse-drawn carriages and the horse-drawn red tram, a novelty for many visitors to the city but which Theodosia refused to go on because it was always crowded. As it was, the stench from the horse manure on the cobblestones was unbearable in the hot weather, even though the shopkeepers and Pera municipality employed people to clean up the mess, which was a never-ending job. A haphazard array of canvas awnings jutted out over the pavements in an attempt to give protection from the hot sun for the customers as they window-shopped, but this only served to contain the foul smells and both she and Electra were forced to cover their noses with their lace-edged handkerchiefs.

Madame Eleftheria's salon was on the first floor of a building near what once the Naum Theatre, which was severely damaged by the Fire of Pera in 1870. The theatre was famous because it hosted Giuseppe Verdi's opera *Il trovatore* before the opera houses of Paris. After the fire, the theatre was purchased by Greek banker Hristaki Zoğrafos Efendi, a close friend of Theodosia's grandparents and a leading banker, financier, and president of the Ottoman capital's tram company. He was awarded by three sultans, sat on the Imperial Board of Estimate, and served as president of the Ecumenical Patriarchate's Advisory Board. In 1876 the architect Kleanthis Zannos designed the current building and gave it a new name –*Cité de Péra* or *Hristaki Pasajı* (Hristaki Passage). Because of his high social status, Hristaki was widely known as Lord Christakis. Theodosia and Alexander had sent Electra to a school for girls in Pera that he also built. A framed photograph of him stood on the piano in the Vasileiou villa, reminding both women of his generosity when they played music.

The carriage drew up in front of the building where the pavement was still being swept. A doorman rolled out a long carpet extending from the doorstep to the carriage while Abdul Agha opened the carriage door to help the ladies step down. A neatly dressed middle-aged woman approached and escorted them inside.

'Good morning, Madame Theodosia, Mademoiselle Electra. Madame Eleftheria is waiting for you.'

They followed her up the winding stairway and entered the salon, where Madame Eleftheria, accompanied by two of her vendeuses, waited for them, their hands clasped in front as a sign of respect. They stood on a large blue, red, and cream Uşak carpet in the centre of the room, its central star motif directly under a glittering chandelier. Large gilt mirrors lining the walls made the room look twice the size. Madame Eleftheria bowed politely when Theodosia entered the room.

'It is good to see you again, Madame Theodosia. I was informed that you require an evening gown for a special occasion.'

'Thank you for seeing us at such short notice. Yes, I have been invited to a wedding and I want something glamorous,' Theodosia said, handing one of the vendeuses her short silk velvet capelet with a silk ribbon, moiré finish, made especially for her when Alexander died. It was one of the first black items she'd ever had made, and although she called it her mourning cape, she grew to like it as people commented on how it suited her pale complexion and auburn hair.

Madame Eleftheria's prestigious couture house was one of many in Pera and Galata, all of them frequented by the fashionable set, but Theodosia preferred Eleftheria's as she felt she had a better eye for choosing the best of European fashions and her taste for fine textiles was impeccable. The salon where she received her clients was dotted with lifelike wax figures in various poses and all wearing the latest styles. Silk velvet chairs were placed in small clusters around the room next to tables on which were vases of flowers and mounds of European fashion magazines. Theodosia and Electra were shown to seats where the morning light streamed through the window, and a young girl arrived with cool sherbets and an array of miniature cakes expertly decorated with the same attention to detail as her clothes.

'How was the Paris Exposition?' Theodosia asked.

Madame Eleftheria's face lit up and she waxed lyrical. 'The Costume Palace displayed garments by at least twenty eminent designers, all members of the *Chambre syndicale de la haute couture*. Their garments were displayed on lifelike wax figures in staged domestic settings. My dear Madame Theodosia, the art of dressing has never been manifested with so much brilliancy. Everyone is trying to outdo each other, and thus, we have costumes of indescribable beauty. As usual, Monsieur Worth's son put on a stunning show, but I am of the opinion that he lacks the creativity and sensitivity of his father, Monsieur Charles. Now he *was* an innovator.'

'I couldn't agree more,' Theodosia said. 'The new couturiers are far more daring.'

Eleftheria handed Theodosia a lavish folio of hand-painted prints depicting garments, each one displayed on a mannequin showing the back and front with its details, cut of the dress, embellishments such as lace or embroidery, etcetera. 'Just take a look and you will see for yourself how exciting fashion has become.' Electra moved closer to her mother as she turned the pages. Aloud, she read the names of the designers underneath each plate: 'P. Barroin, Boué Soeurs, Raudnitz et Cie, and of course, Worth.'

'Take a look at this evening gown by Raudnitz et Cie, described as a princess-line. It has a white taffeta gown embroidered with silver paillettes, and I cannot begin to tell you how exquisite it was. I have my seamstresses trying to recreate it at the moment.'

'May I see it?' Theodosia asked.

'But madame, it is not yet finished and I am afraid its beauty may not be enhanced in such a state.'

'I have a good imagination, and besides, I have this illustration to refer to.'

Not wanting to offend one of her best customers, Eleftheria called over a Greek vendeuse and asked her to go upstairs and prepare the ladies for a visit from Madame Vasileiou immediately. Theodosia and Electra continued to look at the fashion plates for another ten minutes until it was time to go to the cutting room.

The cutting room was as large as the salon and completely filled with mannequins draped in fabric in various states of manufacture. Four enormous cutting tables stood in the centre of the room, and to one side were at least twenty seamstresses, busily working on sewing machines or sewing finer sections by hand. They were mostly Greeks and Armenians, as well as Levantines and several Jewish ladies who specialized in fur and leather. Just recently, White Russians, fleeing problems in the Russian Empire, had joined the staff too. On the other side of the room were the embroiderers, of which there were another twenty. Apart from these, Madame Eleftheria used skilled outworkers too. Until the women walked into the room, it had been a hive of chatter and liveliness; now they all stood up respectfully, their arms at their sides like a line of soldiers, as Theodosia and Electra were taken to the mannequin at the far end of the room. Two seamstresses stood next to it, both wearing padded armbands filled with pins and their arms filled with lace ribbon.

'This is it,' Madame Eleftheria said, glowing with pride. 'What do you think?' She took some of the embroidered sections from one of the women and showed Theodosia where they would go. 'As you see, our gown is similar to the one in the picture, with only a few minor alterations: a lace modesty piece has been added to the bodice on our gown and the sleeves and train are longer. The plate is more extreme in silhouette. Ours has fewer coloured flowers and more sequins.'

'I prefer your version. It's more refined,' Theodosia remarked. 'In fact, it's simply exquisite.'

'I think you will look wonderful in it, Mama,' Electra said.

'Good. Then I shall take it. You have my measurements. Now we must find something for my daughter.'

'Would you like me to make it in black, madame, or dark grey or navy as you are still in mourning?'

Theodosia's reply was sharp. 'Certainly not! I want to look my best for this wedding. Besides, Alexander would not have wanted me to be wearing black forever.'

Madame Eleftheria's cheeks reddened. 'As you wish.' A period of mourning was seen as a sign of respect, but Theodosia was not one for rigid societal rules when it came to dress.

They returned to the salon and continued looking through the plates from the exposition for something for Electra. Theodosia's eyes were drawn to the simpler styles and besides, as her mother, she considered her daughter to be far too young to wear anything too alluring or fanciful.

'May I suggest something from the House of Paquin?' Eleftheria said. 'Some of the designers shown at the exposition, although promising, are still new. Jeanne and Isidore Paquin opened their Maison de Couture at 3 Rue de la Paix, next to the celebrated House of Worth, nine years ago. Madame Jeanne is the one in charge of design and because she was instrumental in organizing the Fashion Section at the Exposition, she was elected president. Mark my word; she will be a big name in couture. Initially, she favoured pastels but has moved on to stronger colours like black and her signature red. Black had been traditionally the colour of mourning, but Madame Jeanne has made the colour fashionable by blending it with vividly colourful linings and embroidered trim. She is also the first couturier to send models dressed in her apparel to public events such operas and horse races for publicity. Things are changing.'

A discussion also ensued between mother and daughter. Electra wanted a dress in a strong French blue, but Theodosia thought it too old for her. Something in pastels was far more suitable. In the end, Theodosia won. Electra would not wear a dark colour, which Theodosia had become tired of: instead she chose a pale apricot dress for her, featuring layers of thin silk tulle and short ruched sleeves.

The bodice was decorated with three-dimensional floral motifs, twisting green vines and small fabric flowers. A peach-coloured ribbon marked the waistline and sleeves and featured prominently in the hemline of the dress, which was decorated with a Greek key design. It reminded Theodosia of the artist Vigée Le Brun's portraiture style. With this simple dress Paquin had bridged the gap between rococo and neoclassicism. The dress was set off by a border of small, meandering laurel wreaths, embroidered into the layers of the gown around the hem and at the waistline. Two more dresses were also chosen as they would need something different to wear for the viewing of the bride's dowry and gifts.

When they stepped outside, Abdul Agha was waiting with the carriage but Theodosia dismissed him. Choosing dresses was an exhausting process and they wanted to go for a coffee before looking around the department stores. 'Meet us in two hours outside Au Bon Marché – and take these.' She handed him a few magazines and embroidery samples that Madame Eleftheria had given them to peruse.

After an enjoyable cup of coffee and a cake in an elegant tea shop on the Grand Rue frequented by ladies of the upper classes, they visited several department stores. Like Madame Eleftheria, the owners had visited the Paris Exhibition and brought back the latest household items. For those who could afford it, there was so much on offer that it was a dilemma choosing what to buy. The first store they went to was G&A Baker, who sold a wide range of goods including textiles, bedding, furniture, and accessories. It was Mr Baker who opened the first department store in the city as well as the first cold store and flour mill. Prior to this he was a gardener and helped introduce to the Ottoman lands lawns and flowers such as wisteria, which Alexander had planted along the terrace of their villa when they married. Here, Theodosia bought perfumed soaps, perfume, and cosmetics. Next door was Carlmann and Blumberg, run by a long-time resident Romanian Jew, where she purchased a fine lace tablecloth. Lastly they visited Au Bon Marché. By the time Abdul Agha came to collect them, they had boxes of purchases and more catalogues. It had been a thoroughly exhausting day in Pera.

After dinner that evening, Theodosia retired to the drawing room to peruse the catalogues with Calliope before making an entry in her diary. She had just settled herself in her favourite chair with her feet on the footstool and was partaking in a glass of sherry when she heard the doorbell ring.

Abdul Agha knocked on the door. 'Madame Hadzigiannis is here to see you,' he said.

Katerina Hadzigiannis was one of Theodosia's oldest friends. They had grown up together and, like Alexander, her husband, Andreas, was a man of standing in Greek legal circles. He and Alexander had worked together, but unfortunately, Andreas died of cancer two years before Alexander. Unfortunately for Katerina, she had been unable to conceive, and her greatest wish – to have a child – did not happen. Katerina was a beautiful woman and had many suitors yet she refused to marry again, although she was known to have the occasional lover. Clad in a velvet cherry red cloak and an eye-catching matching hat topped with a cloud of voluminous greyish white ostrich plumes, she swept into the room and gave Theodosia a peck on the cheek. 'Don't get up,' she said. 'I won't be staying too long.'

Calliope was used to Katerina's visits and knew she enjoyed a drink so without being told, she fetched another glass and poured sherry for Katerina too.

'That will be all, thank you, Calliope. You many retire now. I won't need you again,' Theodosia said.

Katerina took off her hat and cloak and made herself comfortable next to Theodosia, taking note of the catalogues. 'I see you have been to Pera today too. I am presuming it's because of the upcoming wedding.'

'You received an invitation too?' Theodosia asked. 'I am so happy for them. I am sure it will be a most delightful occasion – possibly the society wedding of the year – after the Sultan's own daughter's marriage, of course.'

Katerina took a sip of her sherry, leaned closer, and in a whisper, even though they were alone, stated that she had misgivings about it.

'Why on earth would you say that? Both Ferid Pasha and Ömer Pasha are men of integrity. Why, Ömer's youngest daughter is his pride and joy. Surely he would never have agreed to the marriage if something was amiss? A beautiful and talented young woman and a handsome man with a good future before him! What more can you ask for?'

'My dear Theodosia, you have been in such a state of mourning with Alexander's passing, that I fear you might have missed the gossip.'

Theodosia snapped shut the catalogue on her lap. 'Gossip! You know I have never been one for idle gossip, even when Alexander was alive. Please do explain yourself.'

Katerina had known Theodosia far too long to get upset by her friend's indignation. She shuffled in her chair slightly, rearranging her skirt to get more comfortable before continuing. 'Ferid Pasha sent his son to Paris for two reasons. The first being to further his education, and the second…'

'Go on, I'm listening.'

'The second was because he is a known philanderer. I have it on good authority that before he was sent away, he was trying to seduce someone's wife. His aide in Paris, who is paid by Ferid Pasha himself, reports back about his son's progress. From what I gather, he has not changed his ways in the slightest. If anything, the delights of Paris were far too tempting for him and made him worse. Therefore, his father ordered his son to return and get married before he discredits their good name.'

Theodosia was shocked. Her friend had always had a wild imagination when it came to gossip, soaking it up like a sponge, yet she knew that in this case, she would not have paid her such a visit if she wasn't sure of the facts. Where there's smoke, there's fire, Alexander used to say. 'Oh dear, if what you say is correct, then this is not good at all. Does Ömer Pasha know any of this?'

Katerina gave a deep sigh. 'I have no idea. If he does, he certainly has kept it to himself. It would be shameful to discuss this sort of thing with friends. Maybe he thinks marriage to the beautiful Behice will settle him down.'

Theodosia crossed herself. 'Then we must pray that for everyone's sake, this will be so.'

CHAPTER 2

THEODOSIA DID NOT sleep easily that night thinking of the outcome of such a marriage if what Katerina said was true. In the morning she decided to pay a visit to Hafsa under the pretext of thanking her for her invitation. She did not intend to bring up the troublesome subject, but she would at least be able to gauge the mood in the Pasha's household.

She took breakfast alone on the terrace as Electra was having her piano lesson. The beautiful strains of Debussy's "Clair de lune" drifted through the air from the drawing room, stopping abruptly every now and again when her Italian piano teacher, Signore Salvatini, made her play it again. 'This time I want to hear more passion,' she heard him say sternly. Although she could not see them, she could visualize him gesturing in the air with his fist. 'Passion!' he said to every piece she played. 'Without passion, music is nothing.'

Sometimes he reduced poor Electra to tears and Theodosia would have to intervene. Her daughter was good, but Salvatini, who had studied in Milan and at the Conservatoire in Paris, was adamant that there was always room for improvement. This time she heard him saying, 'Mademoiselle Electra, this music is a poem of much beauty – a journey to introspection – the lifetime adventure of understanding the soul. Play it so.' The music started again followed by, 'Ah, brava, my dear girl. *Much* better.'

When Theodosia had finished her breakfast and Maria came to clear the table, Theodosia asked her to sit down. 'I am going to visit Hafsa Hanim this afternoon. I would like to take a gift and I thought about your baklava. She has a sweet tooth and loves it.'

'Yes, madame; I made a batch two days ago. The syrup will have settled nicely by now.'

'Good, then please prepare a tray.'

Maria's gaze lingered on the thick catalogues from the Paris Fair, and Theodosia asked if she would like to take a look at them. Maria's eyed widened when she saw all the ornate kiosks and new inventions. 'From what I've been told, millions of people have already visited it. Look at this.' She pointed to a full page spread of The Palace of Electricity. 'They say this was fitted with five thousand multi-coloured incandescent lamps. It was a glowing beacon of light and quickly became the heart of the fair and one of the most loved exhibits. In order not to tire themselves out, people were able to move about on movable sidewalks. Imagine that. How Alexander would have loved to have seen it.'

The images were beyond Maria's imagination. She simply could not comprehend it all. Where she came from, people were still travelling by donkey and camels. 'Whatever next! Soon they will be flying,' she said, her mouth curled up in mockery at such excess.

'Don't laugh. They *already* have flying machines.' To prove the point, Theodosia showed her a few and Maria crossed herself several times. 'There are lots of new inventions for the home too. Inventors compete with other to find the next new piece of machinery. Soon there will be new ways to cook and wash the clothes.'

Maria made the sign of the cross again. 'The devil himself invented these iron monsters. If I am going to die, it will be through hard work, not a new invention in my kitchen. Heavens above, surely they won't bring all these...' For a moment she was lost for words. 'These contraptions to Constantinople?'

Theodosia laughed. 'The world is changing, Maria. We all must learn to adapt.'

Maria left the room to prepare the baklava, mumbling to herself about what Chief Cook would have made of all this. 'I am glad he is not here to witness such things,' she said as she exited the room. 'Anyone who tried to replace his cauldrons would have seen him sharpen his knife.' Theodosia laughed.

The tray laden with baklava was put into the carriage by Abdul Agha and Theodosia left to see Hafsa at their waterside yali on the banks of the Bosphorus, not far from the Yıldız Palace in Beşiktaş. There she was greeted by the family's butler and taken to the terrace where Hafsa, accompanied by her sister, Nilüfer, and elder daughter, Ayşe, were waiting for her. A pretty young servant girl carried in the tray of baklava behind them. The women welcomed Theodosia with kisses and kind words about how good she was looking, considering she was not long widowed.

'I try to keep myself occupied,' Theodosia replied. 'Alexander would have wanted it that way.'

The maid placed the baklava on a side table next to an array of other sweets and jugs of fruit juice, making sure it had pride of place. Theodosia had always loved this yali, ever since she was invited here soon after Hafsa married Ömer, the love of her life. After making sure his first wife and two sons by that marriage were well-looked after, Ömer Pasha indulged Hafsa's every whim, allowing her free reign to do whatever she liked with their homes. She had a keen eye for decor and, unlike their mansion in the city, which was decorated in the heavier French style with large sofas, chairs, and tables, as was Theodosia's, Hafsa opted to keep their waterside mansion in the classic Ottoman style. The room in which they now sat was dominated by a magnificent hand-knotted silk carpet from the Hereke Imperial Manufacture, a factory not far from Constantinople that was founded in 1841 by Sultan Abdülmecid I to produce all the textiles for his Dolmabahçe Palace. As was common in the homes of the upper classes, the carpet took up almost the entire floor of the enormous room. In the centre was placed an exquisite Damascene table, large enough to hold enough food for at least twelve people, around which was placed an array of colourful silk cushions, edged with braids and tassels, on which the women sat. A crystal vase had been placed in the centre of the table with sweet-smelling flowers from the garden.

Two maids brought over small golden bowls of rose-scented water and held them as the women cleansed their fingers delicately and dried them on special towels. The towels were taken away and replaced with hand-embroidered towels for their laps, and a light meal consisting of assorted meze accompanied by an array of fruits and nuts was then served. Like Hafsa, Theodosia was brought up to be a woman of grace with good manners, something that was distinguished by the care and delicacy in the way they ate. The food presented was eaten in small pieces with great skill using the tips of her fingers and thumbs, careful not to drop any crumbs. Hafsa occasionally pushed small platters of food towards Theodosia. 'A guest is a cherished member of the family, please take some more,' she said.

When the meal was over, Hafsa said a little prayer and Theodosia made a polite comment. 'May the grace of God be upon you.'

Another bowl of fragrant soapy water was brought over and the women washed their hands again. It was quite a ritual, but one that all women of good standing were accustomed to.

The sun streamed through the open slatted windows in long narrow stripes across the room, highlighting the colours of the beautiful silks in the carpet and cushions in rainbow-like shades that reminded Theodosia of stained glass windows. It was extraordinarily peaceful.

When they had finished, the sweets were served. Hafsa particularly liked Maria's cooking and took a slice of baklava, closing her eyes in sheer delight as she bit into it, releasing the subtle flavours of cinnamon, cloves, cardamom, mixed spices, and orange peel. In turn, Theodosia took a slice of revani soaked in a lemon-flavoured syrup and topped with finely chopped pistachios.

'It's delicious,' Theodosia said. 'Light and moist.'

Hafsa looked pleased. 'By the way, I didn't tell you, did I, we have a new cook. After many years, the old one decided to leave us. This one is of a similar age as Maria. In fact, I believe they know each other.'

'Really! Who is she and where is she from?'

'A small village in Anatolia. They met when they cooked for Master Yusuf, once the chief cook for Sultan Abdulaziz.

Theodosia looked surprised. 'I must tell Maria. If they know each other, I wonder why they never bothered to meet up. I am sure Maria would have told me if they had. What's her name?'

'Zeynep.'

'Does she regale you with stories about "Chief Cook"?'

'No. I've never heard her refer to Master Yusuf as that.' She looked at Nilüfer and Ayşe, neither of whom had ever heard about a "Chief Cook". 'Who is he? All we know is that he passed away a few years ago.'

'Apparently he was their head cook and a very hard man to deal with – demanding; threatened to chop their heads off if their food wasn't up to his exacting standards.' Theodosia laughed. 'Which is probably why this revani tastes so good.'

Hafsa and Nilüfer laughed too. 'We must ask her about him,' Nilüfer said.

The conversation changed to the reason Theodosia was there in the first place – the wedding. 'I must say, it was quite a surprise to hear that Behice was to be married. It seemed so sudden.'

Hafsa glanced across the table at Ayşe, who took the cue from her mother's expression and excused herself, saying she had things to attend to. Theodosia detected a tinge of resentment at being asked to leave. That left the three of them.

When they were alone Hafsa confided in Theodosia. 'We had hoped that Ayşe would be the one to marry first as she is the eldest, but life doesn't always go according to plan, does it?' She sighed heavily.

'The fates are fickle,' Nilüfer added.

Theodosia sensed something was amiss. Maybe Katerina was right after all. 'I am sure she is happy for her sister though,' she said, trying to diffuse the solemn cloud of melancholy that had suddenly settled over them

Nilüfer coughed slightly, her eyes downcast as if she were afraid to say anything more. Hafsa noted her embarrassment and put her hand on hers, assuring her that Theodosia was a good friend and could be trusted.

'I wish that were so,' Hafsa went on, turning back to Theodosia, 'but she was overheard admonishing Behice for accepting the hand of a man she barely knows. In fact she reduced her to tears. We were informed of this conversation when Behice refused to come out of her room the next day. Her maid told us she felt unwell and didn't want to be disturbed. Naturally, I went to see what was wrong and whether we should call the doctor, but Behice refused to say anything, except that she had a headache and would be fine. Her eyes were swollen from crying and I knew it was not a headache. I swore to get to the bottom of the matter and went straight to the maid and demanded to be told the truth.'

Hafsa stopped talking while a maid came in to clear the rest of the things from the table and bring a tray of coffee. When they were alone again, she continued, this time in hushed tones.

'The poor maid burst out crying, saying that Behice had asked her not to say anything and she would be angry if she learned she had broken her trust. Naturally, I told her it was I who employed her and not my daughter. It was her duty to tell me what happened.'

Theodosia felt sorry for the poor girl.

Hafsa sighed. 'When she finally told me what happened, I called in Ayşe and demanded to know why she had been so cruel to her beloved sister, especially at a time of joy.'

Until this point, the two sisters had always got on well, and it seems that the thought of sibling rivalry had never entered their parents' minds. Ayşe was three years older than Behice, a pretty girl, tall with dark looks and sultry eyes which she got from her father. Behice, on the other hand, was a delicate girl with the looks of an angel, as people liked to say. She had her mother's Caucasian looks – green eyes and golden hair – and was the apple of her father's eye because she looked like his beloved Hafsa. Within the family, this fact didn't go unnoticed and Hafsa tried to compensate by showering more love on her firstborn. When word reached Ömer Pasha that his friend Ferid was looking for a suitable bride for his favourite son, Hamid, he naturally let it be known that a union of the two noble families would be a desirable outcome for them all and he immediately thought of Behice.

Preliminary discussions ensued between the two great men, in which other suitors on both sides were discussed and discarded, and when the two men agreed, they decided to inform their families.

When Hafsa was told, she could already see Ömer's mind was made up. Like a good wife, she let him talk first and then brought up several pertinent questions. Why has Hamid returned from Paris so early? Didn't he have a few more years of study to complete first? What would he do and how would he keep Behice in the style she was accustomed to? Most of all, she wanted to know why he had chosen Behice and not Ayşe. 'Why have you chosen our youngest daughter over our eldest? What will people think?' Hafsa said to him. 'Ömer also has another son by his first wife. That son is in the Military Academy with excellent prospects and he is four years older than Hamid and still unmarried. Why not allow our daughter to marry him instead?'

Hafsa was extremely upset. 'There is something else, too,' she told him. 'Ayşe once told me she was attracted to Hamid and was sorry he was being sent to Paris. I think she was hoping he would marry her when he returned. She certainly didn't expect to be cast aside for her younger sister.'

As much as Ömer would do anything for Hafsa, he refused to change his mind about the marriage and, within the immediate family, a dark cloud settled over them. Naturally, they hoped to keep this problem in the family, but people were perceptive, and secrets did not remain secret for very long within their circle of friends. For one thing, the servants overheard arguments too, and started to gossip even though they were required never to talk about the family for fear of being sacked. Even the thought of losing their jobs didn't stop them from eavesdropping.

Theodosia sympathized with her friend and tried to calm her

by saying there were plenty of eligible, handsome men from good families. She immediately thought of a few and one in particular sprang to mind. Aram, eldest son of Narek Azarian, the famous family of jewellers to the sultan, Azarian et Fils. Aram was also known to be extremely handsome, and like his father, an accomplished businessman, but such a union between an Armenian and Turkish family was unthinkable and there was no way that Aram would convert to become a Moslem, although it wasn't uncommon. After all, some of the best photographers were Armenian and had converted to Islam, mainly to improve their social standing in the Moslem community. All the same, it didn't stop Aram from having mistresses of all ethnic persuasions. With a combination of good looks and plenty of money, the women simply adored him. Currently he was rumoured to be having an affair with a Jewish woman, whose husband had died after a mysterious illness and left her a substantial sum of money.

'As far as Ayşe is concerned, this is her fate,' Hafsa said with a sigh. 'It is written on her forehead that she will be married to another man and I am making it my business to find someone good for her.' Nilüfer, who had remained quiet throughout all this, agreed, adding that the sooner the better for all concerned.

'I am sure it will work out for the best and a good man will come along who will be far more suitable,' Theodosia replied. 'Anyway, I for one am looking forward to this happy occasion. Where will the couple live after they are married?'

'Ferid will give them a mansion in Beyoğlu.'

Their conversation turned to some of the guests who had been invited. It was literally, the who's who of Istanbul society. 'Naturally Sultan Abdülhamid II was asked but he has declined because of ill health.' Hafsa fanned herself with her embroidered serviette and laughed. 'That is a great relief to us as I am sure you are aware that he has offended many people in the empire and these days chooses to confine himself either in the Yıldız Palace or the Beylerbeyi Palace. A couple of his consorts will attend though. Bidar Kadin is one of them.'

Theodosia had met Bidar on several occasions and liked her very much. She was described as the most beautiful and fascinating of Abdülhamid's consorts. Tall and slender, with long brown hair and intense green eyes, her beauty was famous also in Europe. Theodosia was married to Alexandra at the time she first met her and recalled one particular meeting which took place in 1889 in the harem at the Yıldız Palace. The meeting was in honour of Empress Augusta Victoria, wife of Wilhelm II. With them was Mathilde von Keller, lady-in-waiting to the empress, who was overheard describing her as "the sultan with a beautiful face but who looked extremely miserable". In October 1898, Bidar met Empress Augusta Victoria again, this time in the grand salon of the Imperial Lodge at the Yıldız Palace. By then, Bidar's importance in the harem had grown enormously.

'Bidar will come with her daughter, Fatma Naime Sultan, 'Hafsa said. 'Also the Grand Duchess Irena Usapova has been invited. She is here for the summer from Saint Petersburg.'

Many more names were mentioned, and although it seemed like a cast of hundreds, in reality there would only be a few compared to other society weddings. This was thought to be at the request of Hamid himself, who was still feeling somewhat embarrassed at being summoned back from Paris. The subject of a gift was brought up, but what do you give to a couple who have everything they could wish for? 'I am sure whatever you choose will be warmly accepted,' Hafsa said.

Theodosia looked at her watch. 'Oh my goodness, is that the time? I must bid you farewell. I've outstayed my welcome as it is.'

Hafsa said she was always happy to see her. 'Allah's blessings be upon you. If anything, I was glad to talk to someone about my concerns. Other than my sister, I have few friends I can truly confide in.'

That evening before retiring to bed, Theodosia took out her diary, refilled her inkwell, and started writing. *My dearest Alexander, today I paid a visit to Ömer Pasha's house where I received a warm welcome from Hafsa and her sister, Nilüfer. She told me things that are quite unsettling and I pray that things will turn out well.*

CHAPTER 3

THEODOSIA TOOK HER breakfast in her room. Calliope brought in a silver tray laden with freshly made damson compote topped with a dollop of yoghurt on which was scattered tiny pieces of pistachio, walnuts, and almonds. It was accompanied by a glass dish containing the finest honey with small pieces of beeswax. It looked delicious and Theodosia tucked into it with relish. She had a sweet tooth and, as a consequence, sometimes worried about her weight, especially in a world where beauty counted for so much. How she wished she could eat like a bird as some women did, her friend Katerina included. Instead, she frequently compensated for her enjoyment of food by taking herself off for treatments at the hammam, or when Alexander was alive, to spa towns in Europe. So far it had worked and she would worry about becoming buxom graciously when the time came, hoping that time was a long way off.

After drizzling honey over the compote and letting it soak for a few minutes, she continued looking through the catalogues with their latest fashions and inventions from the Paris Fair. 'Oh dear,' she sighed. 'How can one possibly choose?' In the end, she put them aside and decided to go back to her usual gifts of something exquisitely embroidered. She much preferred the personal touch.

She took the tray back to the kitchen, where she found Maria pounding a variety of spices with the pestle and mortar. Next to it was a mound of cubed lamb ready to be coated with the freshly ground spices; it would then be fried off for a sumptuous dish later in the day. A symphony of scents pervaded the room – cinnamon, cumin, cloves, pepper, etcetera – all part of Maria's secret repertoire of recipes which she would not divulge to anyone. Chief Cook had drummed that into her. 'Guard your recipes carefully. They are your livelihood.' Maria stood up when her mistress entered the kitchen.

'You'll never guess what I discovered yesterday,' Theodosia said.

'No, Kyria Theodosia. I cannot imagine?'

'Zeynep is here!'

'Excuse me?' Maria looked confused.

'Zeynep – the woman who used to work with you. It must have been when you worked for Master Yusuf.'

'Zeynep,' Maria repeated.

'Yes. What's got into you? Surely you remember the names of those you worked with?'

Maria's face paled. There was only one Zeynep and she remembered her well. She stood transfixed, clenching the cloth on which she'd wiped her hand when Theodosia entered the room.

'What on earth's the matter?' Theodosia said. 'You look as if you've seen a ghost.'

'I did know a Zeynep, but it was quite a long time ago.'

Theodosia burst out laughing. 'It can't have been that long ago. You're not exactly old yourself.' Maria continued twisting the cloth into a tight coil. 'Oh, do stop doing that. You are beginning to irritate me.' She indicated for her to sit back down. 'She now works for Ömer Pasha and Hafsa Hanim.'

'There were so many cooks it's hard to recall them all. Chief Cook hired and fired on a whim, but now that you mention it, there was a Zeynep who arrived one day, but she didn't stay long.'

Theodosia studied Maria's face. 'I thought if you'd both worked together then you might like to catch up with each other on your day off. I am sure Hafsa Hanim would be open to such a meeting – talk about old times.'

When Maria didn't say anything, Theodosia asked her again what was wrong. 'I want to know if anything occurred between the two of you. Something obviously took place because you certainly don't seem happy about catching up with her again. You had better tell me the truth.'

Maria fidgeted with the spices. 'It's just that something terrible took place when she was with us. Chief Cook used to give us challenges. He believed in competition to get the best out of us, but one day – well – that's when it happened.'

Theodosia was intrigued. 'What happened?'

'Chief Cook set us a task – to produce the best dessert possible – something that had not been made before. There were six of us, three boys and three girls, and Zeynep and I were included. We worked so hard that day and when the time came for the tasting, an important member of the household, master of the pasha's horses, was invited to taste them and declare the winner. I recall it was a very hot day and a minor servant of the household was brought in to fan us with his huge fan. It was only a dessert but the ingredients were melting and nerves were getting frayed. However, we did the best we could.

'Then we all gathered round and watched the master taste them. Our eyes were peeled on him and each of us prayed we'd win. He closed his eyes and smelt the delicacies before taking a bite, making noises of rapture and delight that excited us all. The first cook's dessert was declared a marvel, the second, exquisite. One by one, he went through the others with the same gestures. Finally it was Zeynep and I. I was last. After mine, Chief Cook decided to try them himself. He had just taken a bite of mine, when the master of the horses started to feel quite ill. He came out in a sweat, grabbed the chair and, before we could do anything to help, fell to the ground frothing at the mouth with acute muscle spasms.'

Theodosia looked aghast. 'What on earth happened?'

'We didn't know at the time. It all happened so quickly. Someone went running for the doctor but by the time he arrived the poor man was dead.'

'Goodness. Did they discover what it was?'

'Chief Cook was escorted by two guards to see the pasha. The doctor declared it was a combination of a pre-existing allergy and a heart attack brought on by too much rich food. After much deliberation, the pasha, who had never had any problems before with Chief Cook, pardoned him, even though he hadn't done anything. Chief Cook stormed back to the kitchen and in a fit of rage, lined us all up and waved his knife at us. "I will get to the bottom of this, you useless lot. You have disgraced me." He took our desserts, dissected and sniffed each one, particularly mine, which was the last. They all seemed fine. Then someone pointed to the can of rat poison on another bench.'

'Rat poison!' Theodosia looked alarmed.

Maria nodded. 'You can't imagine what he did next?'

'Go on!'

'He lined all the desserts on the floor, opened the door and called the cats to come and eat. We had plenty of cats and dogs around but they were *never* allowed anywhere near the kitchen. He stood back, arms folded, and watched until every plate had been licked clean. And then... Oh, Kyria Theodosia, in front of our very eyes, one of the cats collapsed and died, right after eating Zeynep's dessert. Chief Cook narrowed his eyes, looked at the rat poison and then at Zeynep. "Who was the last person to use this?" he asked in a menacing tone. Zeynep said she was. "The master of the household supplies asked me to put a little in saucers in the storeroom where we keep the flour, grains, rice, and pulses, because of problems with rats," she told him. "I forgot to put it back in the cupboard when you informed us we were having a dessert competition." By this time she was in tears, saying she'd taken care to wash her hands.'

'What happened then?'

'Chief Cook was a quick thinker. If he called the pasha's doctor, he himself would be blamed for not keeping an eye on his kitchen, so he walked up and down the kitchen, cursing under his breath, wondering what to do. Then he picked up his knife again and pointed it at Zeynep. "If you washed your hands, how did it happen?" More tears ensued because she realised she had spilt some near the plate which she was going to use to display her dessert. She apologised as she thought she had wiped everything clean.

'Chief Cook dismissed her on the spot, telling her he never wanted to set eyes on her again. She ran out of the kitchen and I never saw her after that. Until now, I had no idea what happened to her.'

Theodosia looked aghast. 'The poor girl. Couldn't the horrible man see it was an accident and forgive her? After all, the pasha had forgiven him.'

Maria started to sob herself at the thought of it. 'When I told you and Electra those stories about him chasing us with his knife, you thought I was making it up, but he really was an ogre. He threatened us all the time with that knife. "If you ever speak of this to anyone, I will use it – understand?" We all answered in unison – yes, Master Yusuf.'

Theodosia went over and put her arms around Maria. 'What a terrible thing for you all. Poor Zeynep. I am sure Hafsa Hanim knows nothing about all this?'

'Please, Kyria Theodosia, I beg you not to say anything. We all felt sorry for Zeynep at the time. If Hafsa Hanim knew, she would surely sack her.'

'Wipe your eyes. We'll forget we had this conversation. Anyway, I was informed she is an excellent cook, so all must be well. She also told me Master Yusuf died a few years ago, so put it behind you.'

Theodosia left the kitchen wishing she hadn't brought it up. She had met many servants who'd had a dreadful life, and this was one of them.

*

Abdul Agha dropped Theodosia off in Constantinople's traditional shoemaking district in the warren of streets in Gedikpaşa the area behind the fifteenth-century Grand Bazaar. The quarter was home to dozens of small workshops that produced high-quality shoes. She had been using Arev the Armenian so for many years now and wanted to order a pair of bespoke shoes for the wedding. When she entered the premises, Arev treated her like a princess. Tea and sweets were instantly brought and after enquiring about her health and Electra's schooling, he asked what he could do for her.

'I am going to a very important wedding,' Theodosia replied. 'I have already chosen the dress and now need shoes to match.' She handed him a sample of the fabric which Madame Eleftheria had given her and described the dress.

'It sounds exquisite,' Arev replied. 'I will show you some of our latest designs and, of course, we can use the same fabric.' A folio with hand-drawn sketches was brought out together with samples of shoes and fabrics.

After much deliberation, Theodosia decided on a pair of slippers in which the uppers would be made of cream-coloured satin with a bow in the same fabric as her dress. The body of the slippers would be embroidered with floral motifs of silver wire, sequins, and bead. The design of the shoes was open at the back and the toes slightly pointed. They had curved wooden heels, the fashion at the time, and leather soles.

Arev suggested covering the heels with satin and Theodosia agreed. 'And what about a matching purse?' A quick sketch was drawn up using the same fabric and embroidered design. With the addition of a fringed bottom, silver clasp, and chain handle, it completed the outfit beautifully. 'Madame has chosen well,' Arev said. 'Most elegant.' The whole process was repeated again for Electra's shoes and purse.

The next place to visit was the Grand Bazaar, where she intended to spend the rest of the afternoon. She wove her way through the labyrinthine galleries filled with crowds of people looking for everything from food to carpets. At the time she married Alexander, there were over four thousand shops, two thousand workshops, almost five hundred stalls, and even a primary school and small mosque. It was a tradition for manufacturers of the same items to assemble together according to their goods. This made it easy not to get lost in the rabbit warren of stone arches and cobblestone streets. She headed straight for the Street of the Embroiderers. In the heart of this street was a kiosk with inscriptions written in several languages – Refia Hanimefendi – Embroiderer to the Ottoman Court. A gold calligraphy sign in the Ottoman script denoted the workshop was endorsed from the time of Sultan Mahmud II himself and the family had managed to retain it ever since. Inside was like walking into a tent, with giant mirrors festooned with swags of velvet and brocade curtains. A few embroiderers worked there in the cramped showroom, but the majority worked in a separate area behind a screen. Important customers were often given a private tour of the workshop just as Madame Eleftheria did in her fashion house.

Theodosia said she wanted a set of hand towels for the hammam; the best quality by the best embroiderer. 'I would like them to have a nap, rather than a plain weave,' she said. Esma, a granddaughter of Madame Refia, knew exactly what she meant and showed her two types. A smaller one called a *havlu* and a larger version called a *silecek*.

'The main central portion is woven with a pile and we can have three or more bands of alternate weaving of terry and plain at the ends where the embroidery will be,' she said, displaying the long length of fabric over her arm. 'Did madame have any idea of the type of design to be embroidered?'

'I was thinking of a scene of the Bosphorus with houses, the domes and minarets of mosques, and cypress trees – a broad solid band.'

'Wonderful. Please come with me.' Esma took her into the workroom filled with skeins of silk hanging on specially made frames, several drawers of gold and silver thread, and boxes of sequins. The materials sparkled and the hand-dyed colours were so beautiful, it was like walking into Aladdin's cave. Esma introduced her to a middle-aged woman, her head bowed over a large embroidery frame. 'This lady is one of our most skilled embroiderers. She once worked for the imperial court.' The woman kept her eyes lowered out of respect. 'Nihan Hanim, please show Madame Theodosia your samplers.' The woman took out a leather folder containing about thirty samplers of various motifs and stitches, each one separated with fine paper to protect them.

'Your work is exquisite, Nihan Hanim,' Theodosia said.

The three spent the next hour discussing a design, the colours, and the stitches. There was to be quite a lot of gilded metal strip to lend weight to the towel to ensure it fell gracefully when draped about the body, and the stitches would be a combination of drawn threadwork, satin, and random filling stitch. Underneath the main scenic border there was to be a narrow border of gilded metal strip work which would be laid onto the fabric and sewn over with shaded silk. This work would be expensive and time-consuming but she wanted nothing but the best work possible for Behice and was prepared to pay for it. After another discussion about the time it would take, the embroiderer replied that it would take many hours but she would work overtime to have it finished in time for the wedding. Such dedication would be rewarded well, even though it was a strain on the eyes.

It had been another exhausting day but Theodosia was happy with what she had accomplished. In fact she had been so happy she'd almost forgotten about her sad meeting with Hafsa.

CHAPTER 4

A **COUPLE OF** days later, Katerina called at the house when Electra was playing the piano for her mother, eager for her to hear an exercise Signore Salvatini had set for her. It was Beethoven's *Moonlight Sonata*. The two sat with their eyes closed as they listened attentively to the haunting music which Electra played so well.

'Brava, my darling,' Theodosia said when it finished. 'You've excelled yourself.'

'You have come such a long way in a short time,' Katerina added.

Theodosia laughed. 'I certainly hope she has. Signore Salvatini's lessons come with a hefty price tag. He is sought after throughout the whole of Constantinople.'

'Mama!' Electra said, embarrassed.

'Your mother is quite right,' Katerina said. 'Money does not grow on trees. It shows how much faith she has in your abilities. How proud your father would be of you.' She realised she had spoken out of turn and apologised.

'It's quite alright. Alexander was a talented pianist himself. If he hadn't pursued a career in law, he may have been a concert pianist instead. That's where she gets her talent from. It certainly isn't from me.'

'Oh, Mama, don't exaggerate. You play well too.' Electra kissed her mother on her cheek. 'But I do agree with Katerina. I wish Papa was here to hear me play. Signore Salvatini thinks I have what it takes to be a concert pianist. He said he wouldn't waste his time with me otherwise.'

'Well, the signore is certainly one for speaking his mind so he is probably right. Now I think it is time for you to go to your room and concentrate on your other studies, don't you?'

Electra knew that was a cue her mother wanted to be alone with Katerina so she bid them goodnight.

'What a good girl you've raised,' Katerina said when they were alone. 'Pretty and talented. She will make a good wife when the right person comes along.'

'Yes, but she is also strong-willed. There is no way she would marry a man not of her own choosing.'

'Are you referring to Behice and Hamid?' Katerina asked.

'Exactly.' A few minutes of silence passed while Theodosia poured them a cup of tea from her favourite Meissen teapot, part of an exquisite blue and gold porcelain service that was a wedding gift from her parents. She offered her a platter of small cakes topped with swirls of delicate pastel-coloured icing. 'Please do try one of these. They are delicious.'

Katerina chose the pale rose one topped with a sugared rose petal, then patted her stomach. 'I really must watch my waist, you know.'

After a pleasant discussion about fashions and gifts for the upcoming wedding, Theodosia decided to confide in her friend. 'I went to see Hafsa a couple of days ago and I'm afraid to say she is quite sad about this marriage.'

'I don't blame her,' Katerina said. 'Having a gadabout like Hamid for a son-in-law is a frightful idea.'

'No, I don't think it's that. In fact she never mentioned anything about him having had other girlfriends. I'm not even sure she knows about that. It was because Ayşe was overlooked for Behice. Hafsa blames Ömer as Behice is his favourite. More importantly, Ayşe actually confessed that she has feelings for Hamid and is quite jealous.'

Katerina folded her hands on her lap. 'Oh dear, that is not good.'

'Apparently Ayşe had fallen for him before he was sent to Paris, but she kept it quiet until now. If what you say about his womanizing is true, then none of them know.'

'Ömer would know,' Katerina replied sharply. 'He is a man of the world and would have checked up on him. In which case, if he was aware of Hamid's ways, he certainly would have discussed it with Ferid. You know what men are like? They tell each other things they wouldn't tell women – a little indiscretion here and there; all that would be kept between them.'

'You may be right, but why choose when Ayşe is the eldest and already has her heart set on him?'

'As you said yourself, Ayşe kept her feelings to herself, and if Behice is Ömer's favourite, well, that's easy to see why he chose her. Besides, Behice *is* extremely beautiful, even if she is a little naïve, so I imagine he would be hoping that Hamid would change his ways. At the end of the day, a marriage between two influential families is very important.'

A few moments passed while they thought about it. 'You know,' Katerina said, 'when Andreas was alive, he used to confide in me about men like Hamid and the marriages usually ended in disaster. I am sure Alexander must have confided in you too.'

'Yes, he did, and about other cases too: embezzlement, even murder. I recall quite a few of them being in the newspapers. I always felt it was a great weight off his shoulders when he unburdened himself to me. He often used to say, some men are born liars, some are born murderers, and others have been twisted into evil ways, but the law is still the law and when a heinous crime had been committed, compassion is hard to find. We discussed those sorts of things for hours. Sometimes we agreed on things, at other times we disagreed.' Theodosia looked away, trying to hold back the tears. 'How I miss him – and those long discussions. They were always interesting and I often thought I would have liked to have been a judge if I'd been born a male.'

Katerina listened. 'Maybe women will play more of an active role in such things in the future. Who knows? Anyway, my dear Theodosia, there is nothing you and I can do about this marriage except give the couple our blessings and hope for the best.'

'Sadly, you are right. Let us hope Behice's sweetness changes him.'

During the next few days, Theodosia mulled over the situation in her mind. She missed having Alexander to discuss this with. He would have known what to do. It was Calliope who noticed a change in her and asked what was wrong. Calliope had been Theodosia's personal maid since Electra was born and Theodosia trusted her. She decided to confide in her. It occurred to Calliope that Alexander had often used Abdul Agha when he needed "certain information" as he called it. Abdul never quite said what that was but she presumed it was to spy for him when there was a complex issue to be solved and one never was sure who was lying or telling the truth. She suggested Theodosia do the same thing. 'It might put your mind at rest, madame,' Calliope said.

'You know, that's an excellent idea. Thank you.' She went off to find him.

It was eight in the evening and the sun was setting in the west bathing the garden in a glorious wash of rose and mauve tones like the canvas of an Impressionist painting. She found him watering the shrubs. 'Abdul, I need to speak with you.' He put down the watering can, wondering what she wanted as she usually gave him the evenings free unless she wanted to go out. 'Come into the drawing room. I want to ask you something.'

She gestured for him to take a seat next to her. He looked uncomfortable as he was not in the habit of sitting on one of her plush chairs. The kitchen and his own room in the attic was what he was normally used to. 'Would you like a drink?' she asked. 'Maybe a glass of raki or wine?'

'Thank you, madame, but it is forbidden.'

Theodosia knew of many Muslims who drank, even though it was forbidden and she suspected Abdul Agha did too. 'I apologise for being insensitive,' she said.

'What does madame wish to ask me?' Abdul asked, outwardly calm but inwardly feeling apprehensive.

'When my husband was alive, I believe there were things you used to do for him.'

'I'm not sure what you mean.'

'He never actually said but I believe he asked you to check on people for him regarding his work. He once told me that as an ordinary citizen, you could blend in where he could not.'

Abdul knitted his eyebrows together, wondering what she would say next. 'That's right, he did, but he never discussed his work with me, only the specific instructions for small jobs I helped him with.'

'Yes, Alexander was a meticulous man who weighed up even the smallest detail before administering a verdict, and he would never have asked for your help if he didn't trust you. Now I am asking you to do the same for me.'

Abdul's face usually displayed little emotion, but at the mention of his master, tears welled up in his eyes. 'Madame, Monsieur Alexander was a good man, may Allah rest his soul, but surely you are not asking me to spy for you?'

Theodosia smiled. 'Well, let's say I just need a little information, that's all. Like my husband, I too cannot blend in easily in certain parts of the city.'

'What would you like me to do?'

'There's a young man. I want you to find out what you can about him; where he goes when he is alone; who he sees: you know, that sort of thing.'

'May I ask who this person is?'

'Hamid, son of Ferid Pasha.'

Abdul's head jerked back in surprise. 'Are you quite sure? I mean – a pasha's son!'

'Quite sure. I don't have much time either. You can begin tomorrow morning.'

'What about Mademoiselle Electra? I usually drive her to her Italian lessons on a Thursday.'

'She can make alternative arrangements. Calliope can escort her. I will let you know if we need you.'

'If that is your wish.'

'It is, but as it's late, we'll discuss it some more in the morning when we are alone, perhaps after breakfast – by the fountain. You may retire for the evening now.'

He got up and started towards the door. 'Oh, Abdul,' Theodosia called out. 'I have every confidence in you and I trust that this will remain between the two of us.' She omitted to tell him it was Calliope's suggestion.

Abdul bowed, putting one hand across his heart. 'Of course.'

Theodosia walked over to the writing desk and opened her diary. After mulling over what to write for a few minutes, she dipped her pen in the ink and began: *My dearest Alexander, many a time I watched you work at this very desk where I now write, and I listened to your stories with great interest. You were a wise man and I believe*

I learned much from you. Now I see fit to put to use some of the things I learned. I know you held Abdul Agha in the highest regard. He is a man of integrity and I have asked him to help me do something. Perhaps what I am asking of him is wrong, but I am doing what I believe is right. Only time will tell.

*

Abdul was cleaning the marble fountain when Theodosia approached him. She remarked at the beauty of the marble with its meandering fine pink veins that glinted in the sunlight as the water cascaded over the three tiers of fluted columns, tumbling into a large octagon pool that stood in the centre of a lawn. Four wrought iron benches were strategically placed around it, all giving a glorious view of the fountain and the garden with either a view of the house or the Bosphorus and Sea of Marmara beyond the red-tiled rooftops.

Theodosia chose to sit on a bench underneath a jasmine-covered arbor with a scent so potent it made her feel quite light-headed. She indicated to Abdul to come and join her. 'Let's discuss what I'd like you to do, shall we? It won't take long.'

Abdul sat by her side, his posture erect and hands firmly placed on each knee, fingers spread apart.

'As I said last night, I want you to follow Hamid and check where he goes and who he sees.'

'What if he has a bodyguard or manservant with him?'

'Maybe, but if he does, it will be someone he trusts, in which case keep an eye on both.'

'Madame Theodosia, it is unbecoming of a man of my lowly rank to say this and I do not for once doubt your intelligence, but – well, are you quite sure about this?' Abdul was clearly stumped for words.

'It's only for a week or two. I am going to be honest with you. I want to know if he is seeing other women: if he has any mistresses. I hope what I'm asking is simple enough. I may be sending you on a wild goose chase, in which case all will be fine. Indeed, I sincerely hope that is the case.'

Abdul stared ahead digesting the strange request, which he thought was rather dramatic and peculiar, but would never dare say. He already knew Hamid, son of Ferid Pasha, was marrying Behice, daughter of Ömer Pasha, as the conversation in the house was filled with little else other than the grand event, and he couldn't help wondering what Theodosia would do if he did uncover something untoward. She too wasn't even sure what she would do if she found out either. All she knew was that she didn't want her friend's daughter to enter into a doomed marriage.

'What if Hamid realizes he is being followed?'

'If you are discreet, that shouldn't be a problem. Anyway, if Hamid does smell a rat, I will protect you. Don't worry. We'll think of some excuse.' Abdul sat for a while without uttering a word. 'You look so serious. Do you have reservations?' Theodosia asked. 'If so, say so now, because I certainly don't want you to do anything that will make you feel uncomfortable.'

Abdul gave a deep sigh. 'It's just that – well, you know what men are like. Sometimes they have mistresses and it means nothing. Look at our own sultan. He has many wives and concubines.' His face reddened at what he had said and he apologised.

Theodosia laughed. 'It's not only men, Abdul. Women have affairs too. Once a beautiful woman sets her eyes on a man, he loses his reasoning.'

'Very well. When do I begin this task?'

'Today. Report your findings after dinner this evening when Electra has gone to her room. If I need you to take us anywhere, I will let you know. Now, if you will excuse me, I have things to attend to.' Theodosia patted his hand. 'Let us hope he has eyes only for his bride-to-be.'

Half an hour later, she saw him leave the house with the carriage. 'Poor Abdul,' she said to herself with a smile. 'He clearly thinks I've gone mad.'

That evening, Theodosia waited until Electra had left the room before calling Abdul into the drawing room. In such a house where there was always someone present, it was hard for things out of the ordinary to go unnoticed, and Maria, who was busy in the kitchen working on the next day's menu, saw him go in. It was not unusual for Abdul to be called to the drawing room, but she did notice that this time he was there longer than usual and wondered what was taking place. She looked at the clock. He was there for almost half an hour and she was curious. It occurred to her to knock and see whether Theodosia would take her evening milk in bed as she usually did or in her room, but she resisted. That might seem too obvious. Then she saw him leave. He noticed her looking, ignored her, and went to his room. Maria knocked on the drawing room door.

'Come in.'

'Will you be taking your evening drink here or in your bedroom, madame?' Maria asked.

'Bring it here. I have things to do.'

'As you wish.'

When Maria returned, she saw that Theodosia was scanning the pages of several books which had once belonged to her husband. Maria's education was limited but she understood them to be his law books where he'd jotted down notes in the margins. She wondered what Theodosia was doing with them. They were hardly the sort of books she was used to seeing her mistress read.

'Will that be all?' Maria asked.

Theodosia barely acknowledged her. 'Yes. Goodnight.'

Maria returned to the kitchen. She knew something had taken place when Abdul was with her for so long, but what? The next morning at six thirty sharp, he went to eat his breakfast in the kitchen as he usually did. She prepared him an extra serving and, as she poured his tea, happened to mention that he was in the drawing room for longer than usual.

'Allah give me strength,' he said angrily. 'So that is why you gave me extra food.' He pushed his plate away and jumped up. 'Don't make a flea out of a camel,' he said, using an old Turkish proverb. Then he used another, this time tapping his nose. '*Maydonoz olma*! Don't stick your nose in everything.' He indicated to the food she had been preparing and couldn't resist a little dig. 'And make sure you don't forget the pekmez or it will be tasteless.'

Abdul, who was fluent in several languages including French, Arabic, and Greek, always spoke Greek within confines of the family home. This included his conversations with Maria, even though she understood Turkish well, but when he was upset with her, as he was at that point, he chastised her in Turkish. He puffed out his chest and then reverted back to Greek, telling her to mind her own business. He swallowed his tea in one gulp, picked up a piece of bread, and stuffed it in his pocket, mumbling to himself in Turkish as he strode out of the kitchen, almost bumping into Calliope, who was taking the sheets to the adjoining washroom.

A startled Maria stood holding the teapot. 'Oh my!' she said to Calliope. 'What's eating him today?'

Fortunately, Maria understood him well and knew that by nature, he was a kind, gentle man. Abdul too felt bad for chastising her, even though she was a busybody. When she saw him again in the evening, he had calmed down and without uttering a word, placed a rose from the garden on the table. It was a peace offering which she accepted graciously. After his meal, he praised her cooking, saying, 'Ah, Kyria Maria, what would we do without you.' It was as if nothing had happened.

She laughed and waved a wooden spoon at him in the manner of Chief Cook. *Ponirós,* she said with a smirk in Greek.' You are a cunning one.'

As for Theodosia, what he began to tell her worried her. It seemed that Hamid had not changed his ways at all. Now she was in a dilemma. How could she tell her friend she had been spying on their future son-in-law? Both families would blame her for interfering. She waited until Katerina came to see her and told her what Abdul had uncovered.

Katerina's reaction was mixed. The marriage was taking place in a week's time so why had Theodosia done this? What would it achieve?

'It is as I expected,' she said with a deep sigh. 'Let us hope that what Abdul has uncovered is Hamid's last fling before settling down because, my dear friend, to say something at this late stage will break their hearts. We must keep this to ourselves and pray that Behice's love will cure him of his ill ways. That is all we can do.'

Sadly, Theodosia agreed. Her entry in the diary that evening was short one. *My beloved Alexander, what have I done? I fear I have opened a Pandora's box. I wish you were here to guide me.*

CHAPTER 5

TWO DAYS BEFORE the wedding, Hafsa Hanim organized a viewing of Behice's trousseau in their home. Theodosia, Electra, and Katerina went together. A long table had been set up in the large reception room where Ömer and Hafsa held banquets and recitals, and except for three large Persian vases filled with colourful flowers, the table was completely covered with an array of gifts worth many thousands of Ottoman liras. There were porcelain dinner and tea services from France and Germany, vases from as far away as China, silver and gold platters, crystal goblets and carafes from Bohemia, delicate fans made out of ivory with ostrich feathers, cigarette holders with precious stones, perfumes made by the finest perfumers in Grasse, and a multitude of other gifts that both dazzled, delighted, and amused. There was even a mechanical canary that trilled beautifully as it moved from side to side and up and down on its perch in its golden cage.

In the centre of the table were the embroideries, always a great favourite. There was everything the young couple would need, from napkins to bedlinen. Theodosia's towels were there along with bottles of perfumed oils. The guests delighted in closely examining the stitch-work with their eyeglasses.

'Exquisite,' Theodosia overheard someone say about her towels. 'How beautiful Behice will look with these draped around her.'

Behice thanked Theodosia for her gift and, as she ran her hand over them, Theodosia noticed the beautiful diamond ring Hamid had given her when she accepted his proposal. She commented on its beauty. Behice held her hand out, fingers splayed, beaming with pride. 'Thank you. Hamid had it made by Agop Duzian himself.'

The Duzians were known to be one of the best Armenian jewellery makers in the Ottoman Empire. Their family had been in the business for several generations and their designs were sought after by the sultan himself and other royal dignitaries from London to Baghdad. Their designs were equal to anything made in Europe and because of this, plus trading in precious stones, they had amassed a great fortune. Hamid was obviously out to impress when he gave Behice her ring.

After they'd viewed the gifts, Hafsa invited the women to see several dresses, also included as part of the trousseau, which were laid out on a red velvet couch. Only the wedding dress and underwear were not on display. The clothes were equal to anything a princess would wear. Next to them were caskets containing precious jewels, a Koran, a calligraphy set, and numerous other personal objects of beauty, all of which were covered with a fine gauze to protect them.

With everyone so happy, Theodosia reproached herself for prying into other people's affairs. Katerina caught the look in her eye and whispered in her ear. 'Forget it. Enjoy yourself like everyone else.' Theodosia agreed, but she did notice that Ayşe looked rather sullen and went over to talk to her.

'What wonderful gifts yours sister has received,' she said. 'Soon it will be your turn.'

Ayşe nodded. 'Perhaps.' Not wanting to talk any more about the marriage, she excused herself.

Theodosia saw just how unhappy she was. Hafsa noticed the two of them together and when Ayşe left, came straight over. 'You see what I mean. She tries to put on a good face for her sister, but inside, her heart is breaking.'

'You must find her a husband soon,' Theodosia said. 'Maybe then, peace and happiness will be restored.'

'I hope you're right. I've already got a few men in mind. How fragile the heart is. Its heartbeat flutters like a candle flame in the wind, yet is rarely extinguished. Let us hope another candle will burn for her, brighter than before.'

The day before the wedding was a busy one in the Vasileiou household. Calliope laid out the new clothes, shoes, hats, and gloves to be worn by both Theodosia and Electra, which were then inspected thoroughly by Theodosia herself, and the appropriate jewellery to be worn was also selected. All that remained to be done was a little pampering at the hammam with aromatic oils and scented water, a manicure, and their hair styled, which would be done by Calliope. Outside, in the stables, Abdul Aga washed and brushed the white horses, polished their harnesses until the leather gleamed, and made sure the carriage was spotless. Somehow, Theodosia had managed to put her doubts about the marriage and the things she'd learned from Abdul to the back of her mind, and assured herself that nothing would spoil the couple's day.

Even Maria was to play her part. Hafsa knew Maria was an excellent pâtissier, and had asked earlier if she would prepare one of her special dishes and also help Zeynep and the other cooks in Ferid's household on the big day. Maria was nervous: preparing a special dessert for over two hundred guests was not an easy job, especially in the summer when the days were hot and ingredients melted quickly. Everything needed to be fresh so she asked if it would be possible to assemble everything at Ferid Pasha's yali where the wedding was to take place. Their kitchen was enormous and that did not present a problem.

Theodosia asked what ingredients she needed as she would send Abdul to buy them. When Maria gave her a list, at the top were three hundred oranges. 'I need those at least a few days beforehand,' Maria said. 'I must simmer them gently with sugar and vanilla, and then crystallize them in readiness for the filling.'

Theodosia gave the list to Abdul and Maria noticed them deep in conversation for quite a while. This time she would not say anything. Such an occasion did not warrant upsetting Abdul again. The day before the wedding, Maria and the baskets of ingredients were sent to Ferid Pasha's mansion where the wedding would take place. Now everything was ready to be assembled on the big day.

CHAPTER 6

THE MORNING OF the wedding, Calliope woke Theodosia at dawn and opened the windows. 'It's a perfect day for a wedding,' she said. 'Not a cloud in the sky.'

Theodosia closed her eyes and breathed in the morning air, filled with the scent of jasmine and honeysuckle that covered the wall near her balcony. Calliope helped her dress in her new attire, commenting that it was good to see her out of black and wearing the latest fashion again. When the time came to leave the house, Theodosia inspected Electra's attire and told her she looked beautiful. 'You have blossomed into a beautiful girl, my darling. I wish your father could see you. He would be so proud.'

Knowing that this was the first grand occasion since Alexander's death, Electra understood her mother felt a little strange and empty – adrift in the whirl of social activity with no-one to accompany her, and tried to assure her everything would be fine. 'Papa is looking down on us from heaven, Mama. I think he approves.' Her comment made Theodosia's eyes light up, yet she still felt sad at him not being there. 'I will be there for you, Mama – and Katerina. You will see. Soon your sadness will fade.'

'I wonder how many people will talk about me because I'm not wearing black,' Theodosia asked with a cheeky smile.

Electra gave her mother a warm hug. 'You made the right choice. You look quite glamorous.'

They stepped outside where Abdul was just arriving with the carriage. Theodosia clasped her daughter's hand. 'Well, my darling, let's go and enjoy ourselves, shall we?'

The carriage headed for the waterfront at the Dolmabahçe Palace, where a group of guests had already gathered. After an earlier consultation with the sultan, it was agreed that all the guests would be taken across the water to Ferid Pasha's mansion on the Asian shore in the gilded royal barges which had been decked out with flags for the occasion. Not only because the two men were friends, but because his favourite, Bidar Hanimefendi and her daughter, had been invited. The area was roped off and guards dressed in baggy pants with embroidered vests, their swords, guns, and knives secured firmly in their cummerbunds, stood to attention watching to see that nothing went wrong, a fact which only added to the excitement. There was also a small band.

Katerina, looking as beautiful as always, was waiting for them. 'Three barges have already left and I believe we are next,' she said.

Abdul Agha, being Theodosia's manservant, was to follow in

another boat reserved for bodyguards, servants, and maids. In the meantime, the sultan's grooms would take care of their horses and the carriages. Thankfully the water was calm and the crossing would be an easy one. They settled themselves on a soft covered seat inside a long kiosk with deep red satin curtains fringed with gold. Each kiosk held eight people, some of the older women still wearing their yasmaks. When everyone was seated, the oarsmen began to pull away from the embankment, rowing across the smooth water with great skill. Not far behind them was the less ornate barge with the guests' bodyguards and servants. Theodosia spotted Abdul Agha sitting in the front row. He was a tall man and with his dark hair, red fez, and embroidered waistcoat he stood out easily. This was a big day for him too.

Nearing the Asian side, which was lined with some of the prettiest pastel-coloured yalis in Istanbul, Ferid Pasha's pale green waterside mansion, one of the grandest of all, came into full view. The barge pulled up at his private quay, where they were greeted by waiting attendants, some of whom held trays of wine, champagne, and fruit drinks. The women disembarked with great grace, their elegant dresses swirling around their ankles, and proceeded to walk around the side of the mansion to the well-tended landscaped gardens, known as the Garden of Enchantment, discreetly hidden from public view at the back of the house. When they turned the corner they headed towards a large white marquee that had been set up in the centre of a well-tended green lawn, surrounded by a profusion of flower beds meandering up into the hillside dotted with cypress trees. A long terrace decorated with urns and statues at the back of the house looked out on to this spectacular view, and on the terrace was an orchestra playing classical music. Everywhere, servants were walking among the guests, tending to their every whim.

They were greeted by Ferid and Ömer himself and then mingled with other guests until the bridegroom arrived. The wedding ceremony would take place inside the mansion, where the groom awaited his bride. Ferid Pasha's first wife, Gunar Kadin, and her son, step-brother of Hamid, had also been invited. Despite Hateme becoming Ferid's second wife, Gunar and Hateme, mother of Hamid, had been friends for a long time, but as propriety demanded, Gunar and her son politely stayed in the background as it was Hateme and Ferid's day. While the guests busied themselves, Hafsa went inside the house with Hateme, making sure all was in order before the bride arrived.

Theodosia and Katerina chatted with Grand Duchess Irena Usapova, resplendent in a costume made by her own couturier in Saint Petersburg. She was a coquettish woman, known for her infamous love affairs with men sometimes deemed to be below her status, but none of that mattered to Irena as both she and the Grand Duke had an open marriage. Rumour had it that he was homosexual, so these extramarital relationships suited them both as she was quite a Bohemian woman herself, ready to defy convention when it suited her. As befitted such a woman of wealth and standing, she wore one of her many diamond tiaras with a matching necklace of gold chains from which hung more diamonds, rubies, and pearls that simply dazzled in the hot sun. Irena took pride in pointing out that the largest diamond was given to her by a lover who remained nameless.

After some time, an announcement was made that the caïque carrying Behice had arrived. The guests jostled with each other as they stood aside, eager to get a glimpse of the bride-to-be. When she turned the corner into the Garden of Enchantment, accompanied by a retinue of maids, there were gasps of delight. What a sight to behold. Theodosia and Katerina had discussed whether Behice would be wearing the latest Parisian fashion, but to their surprise, she wore a traditional Ottoman outfit – a velvet garnet-coloured dress embroidered with gold and encrusted with jewels. The veil covering her face was held in place with a small diamond-studded cap with a large white ostrich feather, which hung down the right side of her head. On her feet she wore matching embroidered velvet ankle-length boots in the same colour as the dress. She looked radiant.

The procession made its way to the terrace where Hafsa and Hateme now waited. At this point the orchestra stopped playing and Behice turned to her mother for a moment. Both mother and daughter hugged each other before the bridal procession entered the reception hall. It was a touching scene and even Behice's governess and wet nurse stood nearby with tears in their eyes. It reminded Theodosia that someday soon, Electra would also be experiencing her own great day.

The bridal party went inside where the marriage ceremony took place, presided over by the chief imam. Everyone else waited outside with respectful quietness. When it was over, the families came out onto the terrace with the bride and groom, waving graciously to the guests, and Ömer Pasha and Ferid Pasha shook hands, commenting on the union of the two esteemed families. Ömer recited part of a poem by Rumi:

May these vows and this marriage be blessed.

May it be sweet milk,

like wine and halvah.

May this marriage offer fruit and shade

like the date palm...

When he'd finished, all the guests murmured words of praise for the young couple while the best photographer from the highly successful Abdullah Frères photography studio in the Grand Rue de Pera set up his equipment to take photographs of the grand occasion. The studio, run by three brothers of Armenian heritage – Viçen Abdullahyan, later known as Abdullah Şükrü after converting to Islam, Hovsep Abdullahyan, and Kevork Abdullahyan, who were now getting on in years, had been appointed the official court photographers by Sultan Abdulaziz, and as such were in great demand by Constantinople's high society, but this was one wedding they wanted to photograph.

Everyone was happy for the newlyweds. The orchestra started playing again and the celebrations began. The guests moved to the marquee to partake in the spectacular array of food arriving on large silver platters carried by a bevy of servants, and then sat on cushions or chairs to watch the entertainment – a troupe of acrobats, jugglers, and fire-eaters, magicians, and even a dancing bear and monkeys, the latter cheekily snatching food from the guests' plates until a small coin was given to their keeper. Theodosia and Katerina congratulated the couple before going to eat. Behice looked happy, but Theodosia sensed Hamid was putting on a show of bravado and happiness for his family's sake.

'Hamid seems rather distant, don't you think?' Theodosia whispered. 'As if he is acting the part. Maybe it's nerves.'

Katerina, not wanting to allow bad thoughts to enter her mind, said she thought he seemed fine.

'You don't fool me, my Katerina,' Theodosia replied. 'I know you too well. You think as I do.' Katerina chose to ignore the remark.

They took their food outside and found a small table next to a profusion of blood-red roses and settled down to eat: bite-sized morsels made from a variety of meats and vegetables, some wrapped in fine pastry, some on skewers, others stuffed. It was delicious.

'Let our hosts forever be well-off,' Theodosia said.

The summer heat was oppressive and Katerina continuously fanned herself, remarking on what a hot summer it had been. Throughout the meal, they watched a procession of guests going into the reception room where the couple had married to view more presents. Katerina and Theodosia did the same while Electra, tiring of their company, went to sit with another Greek friend of her own age.

The gifts were different to the ones in Behice's trousseau, which were more personal. Most were items of furniture for their new home. Damascene tables and fine carpets, French clocks, and a plethora of objets d'art including fine paintings. Katerina was delighted to see her gift displayed there. She had commissioned the Greek painter Kleopatra Hatzopoulou, student of the well-respected painter Fausto Zonaro, to paint a scene in oils called *Constantinople Straits*. Theodosia had once purchased one of her paintings to hang in her home, but it was another painting among the display which caught Theodosia's eye. It was an oil painting of an orange seller sitting on a stool holding an engraved round brass platter with a few oranges on it. Next to her were two baskets filled with oranges. She wore a simple cream coloured dress over which was draped an embroidered shawl with a long fringe, and on her small feet were yellow slippers edged in gold. The girl had an almond-shaped face and her waist-length, black wavy hair tumbled over her shoulders. Theodosia stared at the painting in disbelief.

'What's wrong?' Katerina asked.

Theodosia checked to see that no one was in earshot. 'I know who she is. She sells her wares outside one of the gates of the Grand Bazaar.'

Katerina looked at her in amazement and then laughed. 'Are you quite sure?'

'Look, that's the Bayezid Gate. The artist has captured part of the golden calligraphy on a green field. It's the sultan's *tughra*.'

'That's true, but how on earth can you say you know her?'

'I'm telling you, I do.'

'An orange seller! How come you remember this girl when there are so many orange sellers in the city: almost one on every street corner?'

Katerina looked closer at the artist's name written at the bottom of the left-hand side of the painting. 'Pierre Maurin. Well, I must say, he has certainly captured her beauty.' Then she stepped back, remembering something. 'Wait a minute, isn't he one of the guests here today? I'm sure I overheard his name mentioned – something about a painter friend of Hamid's.'

At that moment, Hateme came towards them with a friend.

'Hateme Hanim, we were just admiring this painting,' Theodosia said. 'Who is the artist?

The pleasant smile on Hateme's face faded a little, just enough for Theodosia to notice something was amiss. 'He's a good friend of Hamid's.' She took a deep breath which served to enhance her ample bosom even more. 'He is a renowned artist from Paris who studied at the École des Beaux-Arts.' She paused for a moment. 'He's an accomplished artist, but surely there are finer things to paint in the city than' – she raised her head haughtily, her chin jutting out in an indignant manner – 'than an orange seller of all things. Take Kleopatra's work for example, or the paintings of Ali Rıza of Üsküdar. He's dedicated to nature, the Bosphorus landscapes, sailboats and cliffs in his unique style, but unfortunately, he will not sell them to anyone. Not even for a purse full of gold.'

'Subjects like the orange seller are quite fashionable,' Katerina replied. 'They reflect the life of the city that foreigners want to capture. They find it exotic – a little Bohemian. I for one think it quite beautiful.'

'Hmm, I suppose so.' With that Hateme changed the subject and asked if they were enjoying themselves. She then proceeded to discuss the other gifts with her friend.

Theodosia and Katerina took their leave and returned to the garden where the desserts were being served. On the centre table was Maria's special dessert, her spice-soaked and crystallized orange halves filled with a white fondue of sweet-scented orange blossom water, almonds, and walnuts, and topped with thick cream from Bolu. Each one had a sprinkling of vibrant green pistachio nuts and a single rose petal, except for two placed on special platters that were reserved for the bride and groom. These were both topped with their initials in edible gold foil. By now everyone was quite full, but the sight of such delectable desserts was too much to resist. 'Ahhh, such perfection! God bless Maria's hands,' Katerina said. 'They look exquisite.'

Theodosia spotted Abdul Agha, who had been standing in the background keeping an eye on his mistress should she need him, and beckoned him over. 'Abdul, would you be so kind as to bring our desserts over to the terrace? It's far too hot out here.'

'Certainly, madame.' He put the half oranges on two small plates, drizzled a little syrup around them, and took the plates over to the terrace along with two embroidered napkins and silver cutlery. 'Will that be all, madame?'

'There is something else you can do. I would like you to go to the kitchen and thank Maria for me. She has excelled herself.'

He bowed and walked away. Katerina smiled. 'He certainly is a loyal manservant. You are very lucky to have him – and Maria.'

Theodosia laughed. 'I am lucky but they fight like cats and dogs. They think I can't hear them. Underneath it though, they are loyal friends.'

Sitting on the terrace eating their dessert, they watched the people. Some were wandering through the garden, taking in the beauty of the flowers and fountains, whilst others waltzed to the music of Tchaikovsky and Strauss. The sun was getting even hotter and Katerina, who was still fanning herself, complained about the heat ruining her complexion.

Throughout this time, guests continued to go in and out of the house, mainly to view the gifts. A handsome young man walked up the steps and happened to catch Katerina's eye. Katerina nudged

Theodosia's arm when he stopped and looked at her. He smiled and bowed in acknowledgement.

'Excuse me,' Katerina said, 'aren't you the artist who painted the portrait of the beautiful orange seller?'

'I am, madame.' The man looked pleased that she'd seen fit to acknowledge both him and his portrait. 'And if you don't mind me saying, you're most simply quite beautiful yourself. You would make an excellent subject to paint.' His magnetic, luminous hazel eyes flashed playfully and he took a few steps closer, studying her face. 'A fine bone structure with the nose of a classical Greek statue – possibly Aphrodite,' he added playfully. 'Most beautiful indeed.' As if realising his words were inappropriate, he apologised. 'I am so sorry. How rude of me. I'm interrupting.'

'Not at all,' Katerina replied, quite taken with his charm. 'Why don't you join us?'

Theodosia shot her a slightly disapproving glance, but Katerina chose to ignore it. This man intrigued her. He called a waiter over, took a glass of champagne, and sat next to her. 'To your health, my good ladies – and to the happy couple.'

The artist introduced himself as Pierre and told them about his work in the Paris salons. It seemed that he had quite a prestigious clientele. Katerina asked him about his painting while Theodosia watched Hamid and Behice dancing a waltz as onlookers looked on, wishing them a life filled with happiness and many children. At that point she spotted the Grand Duchess Irena go into the reception room. She seemed in a hurry and hardly noticed them. While Katerina hung on to the artist's every word, Theodosia decided to leave them and go for a walk in the gardens. She excused herself, saying she had eaten far too much and needed a little walk. Katerina half-heartedly offered to accompany her.

'No. I shall go alone and admire the roses. You stay here and talk about art with Monsieur...'

'Maurin,' the man replied.

'Ah yes. I won't be long.' As she turned to walk down the steps, she almost bumped into Behice and her maid, who had also decided to go inside.

'I am so sorry, Theodosia Hanim,' Behice said, barely stopping. 'It was my fault. I wasn't looking. I should be more careful.'

Behice's face was as white as a ghost and she was clutching her stomach. 'What's the matter?' Theodosia asked. 'You're quite pale.'

'I feel a little nauseous,' Behice replied. 'I think it's a combination of excitement, the heat, and too much delicious food.'

Theodosia looked worried. 'You must tell your mother. She will be worried. You need a doctor.'

'No. We don't want to alarm her when she is having such a good time.'

Theodosia looked towards the lawn and saw Hafsa and Ömer dancing a waltz.

'She just needs to sit inside for a moment or two out of the heat and then she'll be fine,' the maid replied.

'Alright, but take care.'

The maid looped Behice's arm through hers and continued towards the French doors.

Theodosia was worried but it was not her place to interfere. Whilst others were still eating, dancing, or enjoying the entertainment, she took one of the many small paths that meandered upwards towards the hillside where all types of trees flourished: pine, oak, cedar, gums, cypress, laurel, and acacias. They secluded the gardens below and complimented the incredible panoramic view of the Bosphorus. She marvelled at how many different roses the pasha had, some of which were new varieties with the most wonderful scent. He was even trying to grow the prized black rose from Şanlıurfa on the banks of the Euphrates, but unfortunately, they were never as dark as he would have liked. The best he could achieve was a very dark red. He obviously had good gardeners as by now, the landscape elsewhere in the city was considerably parched due to the hot summer.

At a certain point, she found a seat in a small pavilion next to a fountain filled with fresh water from a spring in the hillside and sat down to admire the outstanding view of the garden and the red-roofed mansion while fanning herself. The guests continued to mill about on the lawn, and Katerina was still chatting with the artist but he wasn't there long before he too went inside and she was joined by Electra and Ayşe. Ayşe chatted for a few minutes and she too went inside. It must be the heat, Theodosia thought to herself. It's a wonder no one has passed out.

Another orchestra took over from the classical one. This time the musicians played traditional Turkish instruments, enchanting the audience with their distinct melodies and rhythms which evoked the essence of Turkey's past and present. The music floated through the air and for a while, Theodosia enjoyed it in the privacy of her floral sanctuary before rejoining everyone else.

On her way down, she saw Ömer Pasha leave his wife's side and go into the house too. As her eyes scanned the beauty of the mansion itself, she happened to spot a figure in one of the upstairs windows. It looked like Hamid and she wondered if he had gone to check on Behice. He appeared to be about to step out onto the balcony when she saw him turn sharply and look back inside as if something had surprised him. He moved out of sight and at that moment she heard two gunshots ring out. The musicians stopped playing and everyone suddenly stopped talking and stared at one another, wondering what had happened.

CHAPTER 7

BY THE TIME Theodosia edged her way through the throng of guests gathering near the terrace, she heard a woman's scream coming from inside the house. In the panic, she saw Katerina holding a fearful Electra close to her and breathed a sigh of relief to see they were both fine. Abdul Agha was with them. Immediately after the shots were fired, Ferid Pasha's guards, now armed and looking quite formidable, assembled quickly to stop anyone going into the house or leaving the property. They acted so quickly that Theodosia was reminded of the fearful janissaries protecting their sultan.

'What's going on?' Theodosia asked. 'I heard gunshots.'

'So did we: they were frighteningly loud and clear. They seemed to be coming from above the terrace on the first floor.' People were looking upwards, their eyes scanning the rooms where Theodosia had seen Hamid, but hardly anyone knew for sure from which area the shots came. 'They were so loud,' Katerina added. She crossed herself several times. 'I pray to the Virgin that whatever took place, no one has died.'

The wailing and screams inside the house only seemed to increase, sending shivers through everyone's spines. People started cursing themselves for saying how beautiful the bride looked; how fine a couple they made; what wonderful gifts, as if they themselves had attracted the evil eye with their words of praise.

Theodosia pulled Abdul Agha aside and whispered in his ear. 'I saw Hamid in one of those rooms. Then he disappeared from view and I heard the gunshots.'

At that moment, Ferid Pasha came out, accompanied by several close male relatives. The crowd went quiet. 'I am afraid I have grave news. My son, Hamid, has been shot and is dead.' The guests all looked at each other in disbelief. Some started crying and others uttered prayers.

Ferid, fighting back the tears, put his hand out to quieten them. 'At this moment, we do not know exactly what happened but the area has been sealed off. The police have been notified and no one is allowed to leave until we give the order. I am sorry to inconvenience you, but I ask that you respect this decision. In the meantime, if you need anything, the servants are here to assist. Thank you.' He turned on his heels and went back inside the house.

His demeanor in delivering this speech showed the character of the man. He was stoic and strong. Katerina flopped down into a wicker seat. 'My goodness, I can't believe it. Do you think its suicide? Surely it can't be murder?'

The words murder and suicide started to circulate through the guests, and although they couldn't believe it either, they started to form opinions, some so far-fetched that Theodosia wondered how they came up with such ideas. Sultan Abdülhamid II himself was one of the first to be informed and after half an hour, the only people allowed to leave were Bidar Kadin, her daughter, and their guards. The sultan decided to send his own doctor, Ismail, and the chief of police, Inspector Ibrahim Bey, another of his close associates. Such was his paranoia that he also sent two more men associated with the Secret Police in case what took place was an act of treason against the state. When they arrived, Bidar left on the royal barge, surrounded by a retinue of palace guards. She was visibly upset at what had taken place.

The men were greeted by Ferid Pasha, who ushered them through the throng to the scene of the shooting. Hateme was kneeling over the body of her son, crying inconsolably. Ferid tenderly pulled her away from her son and asked her maid to take her to her room.

In the meantime, Ömer Pasha was with Hafsa in one of the guest bedrooms taking care of Behice, who had been lying on the bed when the shooting occurred. After Doctor Ismail had examined the body, which was lying on the blood-soaked carpet in his room, he officially pronounced what they already knew, that Hamid was dead. Hateme would not stop screaming and he gave her a strong sedative and then went to see Behice, who was sitting on the bed crying in her mother's arms. He also gave her something to calm her down. Having been told that the reason she was there in the first place was because she was feeling nauseous, he pulled a chair up next to the bed and asked a few questions.

'I felt terrible,' Behice said. 'I only just made it back to the house before I started to vomit.'

'It was probably a combination of excitement and the heat,' Hafsa added, stroking Behice's hair. 'Do you think she may have suffered from sunstroke?'

Doctor Ismail felt her pulse, which was low, and put his hand on her forehead. He said nothing except that she should try and get some sleep for the moment. Such a shock would take a long time to recover from.

When the doctor left the room, Chief Inspector Ibrahim examined the body. Suicide was immediately ruled out as Hamid kept a pistol in his drawer and that was still there – unloaded and still in its satin-lined box, so he couldn't have shot himself. Also there were two shots. The inspector had no other option but to pronounce it murder and asked the police to thoroughly search the room for the murder weapon, but it was nowhere to be found. He told Ferid Pasha he would begin the investigation immediately. This involved speaking with all the guests and every member of the household. Ferid assured him that he had already made sure the property was sealed off. Someone was sent outside and told the guests they would have to make themselves available for questioning. After that, they would be able to go home. If all went well, this shouldn't take long.

'He can't be serious,' Katerina said. 'Look how many guests there are. We will be here well into the night.'

'He's only doing his job,' Theodosia replied.

A desk was set up in the reception room for the investigating team to conduct their interviews. It was next to the bride and groom's wedding gifts – a rather macabre scene, Theodosia thought to herself. She told Katerina and Electra she would go for a walk to get away from the stuffiness of the crowd for a while and asked Abdul Agha to accompany her.

They meandered along the path she had taken when she last saw Hamid. 'This is where I last saw him,' Theodosia said. 'Over there – coming towards the balcony of his room, but he turned suddenly, as if surprised by something. You don't think this has something to do with what you found out, do you?' she asked.

'Let's wait and see, Madame Theodosia. We don't want to jump to conclusions at this stage.'

Theodosia gave a little smile. 'That is exactly what Alexander would have said.'

'I learned much from your husband, God rest his soul,' Abdul said.

'You're right. All the same, I fear that it does have something to do with what we discovered. What am I going to say when my time comes to be questioned?'

'The truth, madame. In the name of Allah, always the truth.'

'And does that go for you also?'

Abdul thought for a moment. 'What is your wish?'

'The same – the truth, but for the moment, just answer the inspector's questions without elaborating. Remember, I am the one that asked you to pry into other people's business, so I want to be there when you tell it.'

Walking back through the garden, they noticed several men poking around in the bushes. 'What are you looking for?' Theodosia asked.

'We are not at liberty to say, madame,' one of the men said.

She looked at Abdul. 'It's the murder weapon – the gun – I know it is.'

Her suspicions were confirmed when they returned to the house. 'The chief inspector told us they can't find the murder weapon?' Katerina said. 'So everyone will be searched when they are questioned. Rather unfair, isn't it?'

'They have their job to do. Until the murderer is found, everyone remains a suspect.'

Katerina knitted her eyebrows together in a frown. 'Dearest Theodosia, I do hope you don't put us in that category.'

The jubilation and joy with which the day had begun had now faded. In its place was despair and melancholy, but they all agreed to go along with the inspector's wishes. 'We have nothing to hide,' many said. 'We will endeavor to help in any way we can,' said others. The musicians packed up their instruments, and the entertainers sat in the shade of the trees reading people's fortunes to pass the time.

Inspector Ibrahim began his questioning with the orchestra, who were quickly ruled out. Then Katerina was called in because she had been on the terrace. At the same time Hafsa appeared in the room with Nilüfer. Their eyes were red and swollen from crying. Hafsa caught a glimpse of Theodosia on the terrace and sent her maid over to fetch her.

'I value your wisdom, Theodosia,' Hafsa said, 'and would appreciate your companionship during this time of grief.'

'My dear ladies, my condolences are useless in on such a tragic occasion. How is Ömer?'

'I have never seen him this way before. He is so distraught, particularly for Behice, and blames himself for the condition she is in. He is so fearful she will take her own life that he doesn't want to leave her. At the moment she is sleeping and he is with Ferid and Hateme.'

Nilüfer wrapped an arm around her sister. 'The police are baffled as they can't find the murder weapon. They've been told to search the house and gardens. It has to be somewhere. Come, let us go and sit in the drawing room, away from all this.'

Theodosia went outside and told Electra to stay with Katerina while she kept Hafsa and Nilüfer company. 'I will be back soon. Don't worry. You're safe.'

Theodosia passed the next hour with the two women in almost complete silence. All Hafsa could say was that Behice's heart was broken. She was so consumed with her daughter's feelings that she barely mentioned Hamid or his parents.

By the time Theodosia was called before the inspector, the sun was sinking over the hillside, casting dark, brooding shadows over the surrounding gardens. Most of the guests had been allowed to leave, having been nowhere near the scene of the crime when it took place, and their names were ticked off the inspector's list. Electra was also allowed to leave with Katerina and would spend the night at her home in Fener. Apart from the servants, only about twenty people remained. Lanterns now lit up the pavilion and lawn, and servants were checking on the remaining guests, giving them tea and coffee.

'Madame Theodosia,' the inspector said, standing up to greet her. 'Please take a seat.' He checked something on his notes and then sat back in his chair. With him was his assistant, Selahattin Bey. 'I knew your husband well when he was alive, God rest his soul. He was a well-respected judge who is very much missed. I wonder what he would have made of all this?' It was more of a statement than a question and as soon as the polite niceties were over with, he got back to the reason they were there. 'I presume you heard the gunshots too.'

'That's right.'

'Where were you at the time?'

'In the Garden of Enchantment. I'd gone for a walk.'

'Alone?'

'Yes.'

'You were among friends, yet you chose to walk alone. May I ask why?'

'It's quite simple. I wanted to inspect the garden. Ferid Pasha is well-known for his love of gardening. He has some rare roses.'

The inspector asked if she minded if he smoked. He took out his pipe and lit it, puffing away, the smell of sweet tobacco wafting through the room.

'So you couldn't have been that far away if you heard the shots?'

'No. The garden curves upwards into the hills, like an amphitheatre, and perhaps for that reason, the sound carries. I knew they were gunshots as they were quite distinct.'

'Most observant – like Monsieur Alexander himself.'

Theodosia didn't reply but she could tell he held her late husband in high regard. The legal system was such that judges presided over their own ethnic groups and Alexander worked on behalf of the Greeks, yet all knew one another and mixed in the same social circles.

'Can you tell me anything else?'

'Yes. I saw Hamid approach one of the first floor windows, as if he was about to look outside. Then he seemed distracted by something and went back in. That's when I heard the gunshots.'

The inspector's eyes widened. 'That is indeed interesting. Were you aware it was his bedroom?'

'No. I have never been upstairs so have no idea where the bedrooms are.'

'The fact that you use this word – distracted – do you think he knew someone else was in the room? It seems from this statement that he may have seen the murderer.'

'If he was shot from the front, then in all likelihood he would have seen the perpetrator, but I have no idea if that person was already in the room.'

'Hmm! The murderer obviously knew Hamid was there though.'

'It does seem that way.'

Inspector Ibrahim puffed on his pipe a little more, mulling things over in his mind. 'Our beloved sultan is worried that the bullets might have been intended for Ferid Pasha given that he is a military advisor to the government. We have many enemies, you know, and we must rule that out. Maybe the perpetrator was intending to kill the pasha. What do you say to that?'

Theodosia was aware there *were* political upheavals taking place in the empire but it wasn't something that had occurred to her. 'Inspector, I am of the opinion that if someone was going to kill the pasha, they wouldn't have done it at his son's wedding and they certainly wouldn't have shot his son instead.'

'But what if this person opened the door thinking that the pasha was inside the room, and then realised it was Hamid instead and shot him purely because Hamid saw him with a gun?'

'Have you checked where the pasha was at the time? I suggest that he was with his wife or the guests, so I cannot agree with that hypothesis, sir. I believe that whoever did this meant to kill Hamid and no one else.'

The inspector smiled. 'I can see you have an analytical mind.'

At that moment two policemen came into the room and called him aside. After a short conversation he returned to his desk and let out a deep sigh. 'It seems they still cannot locate the murder weapon and as it is getting late, if you don't mind, I must conclude our little chat. You may go home now.'

'Thank you. Will that be all?'

'For the moment, yes. I know you live in Teşvikiye. Would you mind if I called by to speak more with you if I have additional questions?'

Theodosia said she would be only too happy to help in any way she could. After saying goodbye to her hosts, she left the house with Abdul Agha and took the barge back across the water. Maria was not with them as all the staff was required to stay in the house for further questioning.

Throughout the journey home, Theodosia asked Abdul what he'd said to the inspector. He replied that he'd been outside when he heard the shots, but both he and Theodosia knew that if it would help solve the case, they would have to tell the inspector what had been going on. Theodosia made her own bedtime drink that night and was too exhausted to write in her diary, but as it was her way of communicating with Alexander, she made an effort.

My darling Alexander, what a day it has been. From great joy to utter sadness. Ferid Pasha's son was murdered and I fear that this has something to do with the Pandora's box I opened. I will draw on your strength and wisdom and do what I can to help, as you would have expected nothing else from me. Your loving Theodosia.

CHAPTER 8

Electra returned home from Fener the next day still in a state of distress, so Theodosia cancelled her daughter's lessons for a week and told her to rest. Calliope would be on hand to attend to her. That was easier said than done. A murder is not something one pushes to the back of the mind. She would suffer from nightmares for weeks to come.

Maria did not return home until the following day, saying that the staff had all been questioned too. Neither Chief Inspector Ibrahim nor anyone else told them what was going on, except to say that they were looking into Behice's illness. Because of her sickness, none of the food was to be cleared away either as the police needed to inspect what was left over. With food still left out, in the hot weather, the smell was becoming unbearable. After being interviewed, Maria was allowed to go, but told to make herself available should there be more questions.

'Where do they think I will go?' Maria said miserably. 'We were all treated like suspects and I don't understand what this has got to do with us? We are just cooks.'

'The police have their job to do, Maria. Surely you want to know who murdered Hamid too?'

'Of course, but why suspect us of foul play? Behice was the only one to be ill.'

Theodosia sympathized. 'At the moment, no one knows what to think. Imagine the families' distress. It will be in the newspapers by now. All of the empire will hear about it.'

Theodosia gave Maria a day off. 'Get some rest and don't bother about preparing food for us.If we need anything, Calliope will help, but for the moment, food is the last thing on our minds.'

It was the day after when Inspector Ibrahim paid her a visit. By then the murder had made headlines, not only in the Ottoman Empire, but in foreign newspapers too. Reports of Hamid's death had been noted by all the foreign diplomats, who, like the sultan, feared it had something to do with political unrest. In the meantime, Theodosia had already had a long discussion with Abdul Agha and it was decided that if it would help bring the perpetrator to justice they must tell the inspector what they knew about Hamid's secret life. Perhaps it had nothing to do with the murder at all, but it was still better that he knew.

Inspector Ibrahim kissed the back of Theodosia's hand in a gracious manner. 'I am extremely honoured to be in your company again.'

Theodosia showed him into the drawing room. 'Please take a seat. If I can be of assistance in any way, I am only too happy to help.'

The inspector sat opposite Theodosia in Alexander's favourite armchair, his back erect, his black hair gleaming and slicked back, and not a hair in his finely clipped goatee beard out of place. His demeanor was official, calm, and collected, as he removed his file from his briefcase and opened it at a page filled with notes. Theodosia noted his handwriting was exceptionally small and neat. Just like the man himself.

Maria, who by now had resumed her duties, served them coffee and biscuits along with a jug of water and a bowl of orange-peel spoon fruits. The inspector declined the fruits, patting his stomach and saying he was watching his weight. On seeing him again, Maria was nervous, but the inspector put her at ease, saying he wasn't going to bite her head off. His words did not make her any more relaxed, but she managed a nervous smile.

What can I do for you?' Theodosia asked. 'Are you any closer to solving the murder?'

'At the moment I admit to being nowhere near solving it. I do have a few suspicions but that is only because of people's behaviour – such things as a murder can cause people to react in surprising ways. So, I confess I need a few more facts first. That is why I came here.'

'I'm afraid I am not qualified in police or judicial matters. I only have my late husband's experience to guide me on these matters, so I'm not sure what else I can tell you, except that which I saw on the day which was very little.'

The inspector sensed Theodosia was holding something back and wondered if it was due to Maria's presence, so he decided to wait until they were alone again before continuing the conversation. He commented on the coffee. 'Ah, perfect. Madame Maria makes excellent coffee. It is an art, you know.' He took another sip, letting the taste linger a while.

'Have you any idea at all who committed the crime?' Theodosia asked when they were alone. At the same time, she spotted Abdul Agha in the garden pruning the roses. He momentarily glanced towards the window.

The inspector put his cup down and studied her. With the morning sun shining on her face, he noted how much younger she looked than in the sepia-tinted photograph of her thatAlexander had kept on his desk in his office. He'd admired it many times when they'd worked on a case together, but it didn't do her justice. Someone will ask for her hand in marriage soon, he thought to himself: someone who appreciates a woman with brains, beauty, and elegance. She's far too good a catch to be alone for the rest of her life. That would be a tragedy.

'I am fully aware that both families are friends of yours,' the inspector replied, 'but I ask as a trusted friend of your late husband, if you are aware of anything, no matter how small, that might help us, please tell me. None of us want to see Hamid's murder go unpunished.' There was a short pause and then he gave a deep sigh. 'I will be honest with you, Madame Theodosia, I don't know why, but my instincts – which I might add can be very useful in my occupation – tell me you know more than you are letting on.'

Theodosia thought he sounded like Alexander, who also trusted his instincts. 'The last thing I want is to be is to be thought of as a gossip-monger.' She blushed. 'What I am trying to say is that if I *do* tell you something – it may or may not be useful.'

'Madame, let me be the judge of that. I also swear on the holy Koran that whatever you tell me will remain in confidence.'

Theodosia was also a good judge of character herself and could tell he meant it.

'It may take quite a while to explain.'

'I have all the time in the world.' Inspector Ibrahim relaxed a little as if making himself comfortable for what she was about to say.

'May I ask you something first?'

'Of course.'

'What about the gun? Have you found it?'

'Ah, yes – the gun! Please forgive me, but I was about to tell you that before I asked for your cooperation.' He pulled out a photograph from his file and showed her.

'This is a beautiful pistol with unusual features, particularly the mother-of-pearl grip,' Theodosia said.

'You know about these guns?' the inspector inquired.

'Of course. It's called a Velo-Dog – a pocket revolver which is often used by both men and women as a defense for cyclists against dog attacks. My husband had one, and I recall we took it with us on a trip to Bursa. For a woman they slip easily into a purse or pocket, and for a man, his waistcoat.' Theodosia looked at the photograph again. 'Who does it belong to? Is this the murder weapon?'

'It's Hamid's, and no, it's not the murder weapon. This one still has all the bullets in the chamber. After searching the house again, we found it in one of his coat pockets, *but* the one that was fired *was* similar to this – a pocket gun. These guns are attributed to the Belgian arms maker Jacques Mussen-Lallemand, who produced them between 1894 and 1897. It's chambered in 5.75mm and features a unique swiveling ejector rod and folding trigger. This particular design was produced for the Ottoman market. It has a small star and crescent stamped on it. We've checked with two importers here and their records say they sold quite a few but cannot recall selling one to anyone in Ferid Pasha's household. It has not been helped by the fact that there was a fire in one of the factories a few years ago which destroyed a lot of the paperwork. His father said Hamid owned several guns and may have purchased this in Paris.'

Theodosia looked at the picture carefully. 'That's interesting, but what does that tell you if it's not the murder weapon?'

'As you so cleverly pointed out before, this means the murder weapon could belong to a man *or* a woman.' There was a slight pause. 'You were going to tell me something.'

'Yes. Would you please excuse me for a moment?'

She went outside to speak to Abdul; he was a shy man at the best of times, but being in the presence of the police made him particularly nervous. Theodosia told him to calm down. 'Inspector Ibrahim Bey is a good man. We'll just tell him what we know, that's all.'

Inspector Ibrahim looked surprised when she returned with her manservant and asked him to take a seat next to them.

'It's like this,' Theodosia began, and proceeded to tell him about Katerina saying she'd heard Hamid was brought back from France because his father deemed him to be an idle spendthrift with a penchant for women, in many cases women of ill repute. 'This was why he was to marry and settle down as soon as possible. It was his father's wish, not his. If he didn't do what he was told, Ferid Pasha would disown him.'

The inspector nodded. 'I'd heard something of the sort myself, but do carry on.'

'At first I thought the marriage between two eminent families a wonderful idea, but after hearing this, I became worried when I heard that he was to marry Behice, who is... Well, how can I put it? She is extremely soft and of a delicate disposition – naïve is the better word. I was of the opinion that a woman with a stronger personality might suit him better. Both families are long-time friends of mine –Hafsa, in particular – and I could see she wasn't too happy about it. I am sure it probably wasn't the right thing to do, but I asked Abdul to spy on Hamid.'

'Spy!' The inspector looked perplexed. 'May I ask why, and what you were going to do with your information?'

Theodosia felt like an irresponsible child. 'Maybe the word "investigate" is more apt. I know it seems silly, but I was aware that Alexander sometimes did this when he needed information that was not forthcoming.' She looked the inspector straight in the eyes. 'I am sure, Inspector, that you too have resorted to such things yourself at times.' He moved uncomfortably in his chair. 'So I asked Abdul to do what he did for my husband. It's as simple as that.'

'*Investigate*, you mean?'

'Yes.' She turned towards Abdul, who was still embarrassed by the situation. 'Abdul, please tell Inspector Ibrahim what you found out.'

The next hour was taken up with Abdul's account while the inspector made copious notes.

'When Hamid returned from Paris, he was living at his parents' city home in Akaretler in Beşiktaş, only visiting the yali at the weekends. At Madame Theodosia's request, I watched the pasha's house for several days – in fact it was almost two weeks. It's in a leafy cul-de-sac and partially hidden from view due to the large gate and tall hedge. Luckily, there is only one way to enter or exit the street. On the corner, at the junction of a busier street, there is a cluster of small coffee shops and I spent time in there, playing backgammon and cards while keeping a watch on whoever passed from the house

'It soon became clear that his regime was to leave the house around midday, usually in his carriage. That's when I started to follow him. During the first few days he was in the habit of taking lunch in a tavern near the Grand Bazaar and then he would walk to a nearby han where there was a hashish café. To all intents and purposes, it looked like an ordinary hashish café, with seating around the walls, silk cushions, and narghiles, but this was no ordinary café. Adjoining it was a wooden door with a small square grill which was opened from the inside by someone checking on the customers. When someone entered that door, they went to Paradise. Not the one after death, but the one sought after by the living. It was an opium den and a brothel.'

'How do you know this?' the inspector asked.

'Because directly across from the han was a carpenter who made chairs, stools, brooms, and delightful birdcages, one of which I purchased for Madame Theodosia and which hangs on the terrace – although as yet, there is no bird in it – told me so.'

'I see. What else?' the inspector asked, knowing that men of all echelons of society were acquainted with prostitutes at sometime or other – himself included. His cheeks reddened when he thought of it as he was certainly not there in the line of duty.

'It was the carpenter who told me distinguished men visited it, including foreigners.'

'So Hamid visited prostitutes. That is not a crime?'

'You are right, Efendim, but it wasn't the only thing he did. I noticed that he took a shine to the orange seller who sat outside the Bayezid Gate. He used to chat to her on his way there and back.'

'That is also not a crime.'

'No, but a few days after he took her to a small hotel, a seedy place, about a kilometre away. They were there quite a few hours. After they left, just to be sure they were together, I paid the hotel manager a few pounds and he told me they paid for one room and it was not the first time they'd been there. In fact, he kept that room especially for the customer in question.'

Theodosia thought of the wedding gift and asked the inspector if he'd seen the painting.

'Yes. I did. A beautiful woman: probably about seventeen or eighteen years old.'

Theodosia could tell that he still was not convinced this had anything to do with the murder but she persevered. 'You know, don't you, that if such a woman was discovered to be having an affair, this would be frowned upon?

'Maybe she is not a Muslim, madame. Maybe she is Greek, Jewish, Armenian, or a refugee from the empire down on her luck, looking for any way to make a living. Maybe Hamid paid her.'

'She is certainly Turkish, Efendim,' Abdul said. 'She has an accent which I believe is from the provinces. You can also tell by the way she dresses that she is Turkish. She occasionally covers her head with a veil – which I might add, frequently slips to reveal her beauty.'

'You spoke to her then?'

'Yes, on more than one occasion. The first time I bought a few oranges from her for Madame Theodosia, in order to engage in a conversation, but I didn't find her talkative. In fact I found her to be quite shy.'

'But not shy enough to spend time with a man alone?' Inspector Ibrahim said, his voice tinged with disapproval. 'That area is filled with people, so she obviously wanted to be with him. Who took care of her oranges while she was away? Someone must have known what she was doing. A woman trying to eke out a living selling oranges just doesn't get up and leave.'

Abdul looked towards Theodosia for support.

'It is something that we ourselves discussed,' Theodosia replied. 'She was probably doing it for money. You know how poor some of these people are. Besides, she would have known Hamid was a man of means and she couldn't possibly be with him on a permanent basis.'

'You didn't answer my question.'

'I believe her friend who was also a vendor watched her stand for her,' Abdul said.

'Was she wearing a wedding ring?' the inspector asked.

Abdul said not, even though many young women of her age were married.

The inspector finished writing this down and let out a deep sigh. 'This is still not a crime, and please forgive me, but I fail to see where this is leading, except that it doesn't make Hamid look like a man of good character.'

'You are quite right,' Theodosia added. 'But apart from this liaison, he was also seeing another woman, this time a lady more in keeping with his social standing. This particular lady, he wined and dined at the Pera Palace hotel.'

The inspector raised his eyebrows. 'Do you know who it was?'

She turned to Abdul, who continued with his story. 'You will appreciate that a man of my standing would not think of going inside such an establishment as the Pera Palace on my own, so I was unable to ask questions. What I can tell you though, is that this woman arrived by ferry from Büyükada and was always met by Hamid, who was waiting with his coach. I know of two times that she spent the night with him at the hotel.'

'And you didn't catch sight of her when she got off the ferry?'

'I'm afraid not. She always wore a travelling cloak with a hood that covered her face and hair, so I don't even know what colour it was. She got straight into his carriage and they drove away. She walked with grace and, underneath the cloak, her clothes and shoes were those of an elegant woman with good taste.'

'What colour cloak did this lady wear and what was the colour of her shoes?'

Abdul Agha thought about it for a minute or two. 'I believe the cloak was a rich chocolate colour, and the shoes – I think they were mauve or a reddish brown. I can't quite recall.'

Theodosia quickly let it be known that Abdul was accustomed to always seeing such women, because of their guests or when he took her to the dressmakers and embroiderers. 'I think that this liaison shows that Hamid also seduced women of means too: someone who was his equal.'

'Quite a Casanova!'

'I think we would all agree on that,' Theodosia replied.

'Did you note the days this woman stayed at the Pera Palace, Abdul?'

Theodosia went to her diary and gave him the exact dates.

'That is at least something. We can check out who the guests were on those days.'

The inspector looked at his watch. He had already been there an hour and made pages of notes.

'The inspector must be quite hungry by now, Abdul,' Theodosia said. 'Would you please go and tell Maria to bring more coffee?'

'Thank you, Madame Theodosia, but I really must be on my way.'

'There is something else you need to know. Surely you can stay a little while longer.'

Inspector Ibrahim turned another page in his notebook, pen poised.

'There was another guest at the wedding who I found quite intriguing – the artist who painted the orange seller. He is – was – a friend of Hamid's. They knew each other very well in Paris. Abdul, you said that Hamid took the artist, a man by the name of Pierre Maurin, with him sometimes and it seems he may have taken quite a shine to the girl.'

'That's understandable,' replied Ibrahim. 'She's beautiful and, as an artist, he would have an eye for a good subject.'

'I agree, particularly as oriental subjects are much sought after by Europeans these days.'

'Has the artist painted other such subjects?'

'I don't know. He came from Paris soon after the marriage was announced and stayed with Hamid in his house. Apart from that, I know nothing else about him.'

Abdul returned, followed by Maria. She set the tray down and poured them their coffee. 'Will that be all, madame?' Maria asked.

'Not unless the inspector has any questions for you.' She turned to Ibrahim with an enquiring look.

He took a good look at Maria, as if recalling her from his earlier interview at the time of the murder. 'For the moment I have enough to follow up on.'

Maria gave a little curtsy and left the room, grateful to be away from any more unsavory questions. Looking around to check that Calliope or Electra were nowhere in sight, she put her ear to the door and listened. When she didn't hear her name being mentioned, she returned to the kitchen.

'Unless you have anything else to add, I'll be on my way.' He went through his notes carefully. 'One thing though. Who do you know who lives in Büyükada?'

Theodosia laughed. 'Inspector Ibrahim, you might need another notebook if I answer that question. It's such a beautiful island that almost all the wealthy families either have another home there or visit for holidays. This includes Turks, Greeks, Jews, Armenians, and Levantines – everyone of means.'

'As I said, I will check out some of these things, but I have to be honest, I can't see that any of what you've told me would lead to a murder.'

While he drank his coffee, they chatted about the weather, the garden, and anything but the murder. He thanked them both for their time and left.

'Well,' Abdul said, after he'd gone, 'he struck me as if he thought we were leading him on a wild goose chase.'

At this point, Theodosia had deliberately left out Ayşe's jealousy and the fact that Hafsa had been against the marriage from the beginning. That sort of thing happened in most families.

'Let's see what he comes up with,' she replied. 'He's an astute man and I am sure that he will solve Hamid's murder sooner rather than later. At least he knows the gun used was similar to Hamid's.'

CHAPTER 9

AFTER ALLOWING THREE days of mourning, Theodosia visited Hafsa again to see how Behice was. Hafsa looked pale and tired, as if she carried the weight of the world on her shoulders. It was no longer the happy home it used to be. Instead, it was shrouded in a combination of disbelief, sadness, and anger.

'Behice's sickness was never diagnosed,' Hafsa said, 'but Allah be praised, she recovered after a few days in bed, mostly sleeping due to the medicine the doctor gave her. Now she's up and about and eating once more. However she's not herself, as you can imagine.'

'Hamid's death – how is she taking it?' It seemed such a silly question, but one that had to be asked.

'It's as if it's not sunk in, but I know my daughter well and I see that the bright light of youth has gone from her eyes. She seems distant – almost devoid of emotion – and that scares me. The doctor thinks its delayed shock and when it sinks in, there will be an outpouring of grief and we must be there for her. He even recommended a sanatorium where she could get psychiatric help. When I said no, he assured me that there were new thoughts on psychiatry and mentioned a European by the name of Sigmund Freud who was having success with his patients.'

Theodosia already knew of Freud from Alexander's studies, but was also aware that new ideas in psychiatry were still in their infancy and not everyone agreed on the new treatments, especially when it came to the insane. 'Behice is not insane,' Theodosia replied. 'Far from it. She has a loving family. I'm sure that will help her better than any sanatorium. How is everyone else – Ömer, Ayşe?'

'Ayşe is sullen and seems not to care about her sister anymore. She refuses to talk about it or even comfort her sister, which also worries me immensely. Hamid is dead – there's nothing we can do about it now – so she must put her jealousy behind her and be there for her sister. As for Ömer, well, what can I say? He is constantly talking with the police and is upset that there is still no suspect. He comes home and wants to be left alone. I have tried my best to console him, but he gets angry, telling me that he will kill the murderer himself when he finds out who it is.' Tears streaked down her cheeks. 'I am trying to keep my family together but it's a struggle.'

Theodosia put her arm around her and told her whenever she needed her, she was there for her. 'The inspector came to see me and showed me a photograph of the type of gun used. Surely that won't be too hard to trace.'

'He showed us too, but what good is that if it is not the actual murder weapon?'

There seemed little more to say and because the mood in the house was so uncomfortable, Theodosia returned home. She did think about visiting Hateme and Ferid, but as it was their son who was murdered, she thought their grief would be too much to bear at the moment. Instead, she decided it more appropriate to wait until after the funeral, which had been delayed because of the autopsy.

Over the next few days, she anxiously tried to keep herself occupied while waiting for Inspector Ibrahim to return. Once a month, she and a group of friends gathered together at someone's home for their embroidery session. There were many such societies and groups in the city, but she had been a member of this one since she was a teenager. They called themselves the Embroidery Sisters and all the members were from a cross-section of Constantinople's wealthy families – Turks, Greeks like herself, several Jewish women, Levantines, and a few foreign wives whose husbands worked for the Diplomatic Corps or foreign enterprises, or who were teachers. This time it was Theodosia's day to host them and she had completely forgotten all about it. It was Calliope who reminded her that they were due in a few hours' time.

'Oh my goodness, I had so much on my mind, I completely forgot. Has Maria prepared food for them?'

'It's all taken care of,' Calliope replied. 'Where will you sit today?'

'It's such a beautiful day, far too stuffy to sit inside, so I think we'll go on the terrace.'

Calliope went to the kitchen and informed Maria where the ladies would be sitting and asked if she could she arrange the table and seating. 'Make sure the vases are filled with colourful flowers,' she added, 'to cheer everyone up.'

Theodosia went upstairs to her room and discussed with Calliope what to wear. As all her friends dressed with fashionable elegance, even though it was only an embroidery group, Calliope suggested something beautifully fitting for the occasion – a flattering two-piece ensemble made of blue silk with a swirling pattern of dots, and trimmed with lace at the hem, wrists, and shoulders. Theodosia agreed. The shoulders and wrists were decorated with black ribbon, and the front of the bodice showcased an alternating pattern of striped silk ribbon and chiffon. She wore her hair in a soft voluminous style known as the Gibson girl hairstyle, considered to be the beauty ideal popular in the latest magazines she read. Calliope was an expert at this style and did it in no time at all.

'What would I do without you?' Theodosia said when she looked at herself in the mirror. 'You make me look like a film star.'

That brought a smile to both their faces and lightened the atmosphere.

Usually, there would be about ten ladies in attendance at an embroidery session, but that day there were sixteen. Theodosia wasn't in the least surprised. She knew some of them were there to find out what took place at the wedding. They arrived with their embroidery frames, hoops, bags of gold and silver thread, and colourful skeins of silk, and quickly spread themselves out on large soft cushions that Maria had strewn around the terrace. She had been careful to space them out so that everyone could work without bumping the frames or mistaking the threads of other embroiderers. The seating arrangement also enabled them to hear what everyone was saying while working.

After quenching their thirst with cool fruit drinks, cleansing their hands in sweet-scented orange blossom water, and checking each other's work, they soon settled down to work. Theodosia picked up her own hoop and continued embroidering a flowing stem design with roses, verbena flowers, and buds worked in couching or ribbon-work. It would later be sewn into the bodice of a dress. Others either worked on their own designs for the home or for their children's dowries. It was quite a diverse group and all were accomplished, having been tutored in the revered art of embroidery from an early age.

In the hot afternoon sun, needles and silver and gold thread glinted as the dextrous embroiderers worked away, shading their motifs with a rainbow of colours until trees and flowers sprang to life, blooming like spring blossoms on their frames. After a while, the conversation turned to the wedding and the murder, which wasn't exactly a surprise for Theodosia. By now, the newspapers reported on it daily, showing photographs of Hamid or Ferid and Ömer Pasha. Thankfully, they had not posted one of Behice. The general question was were they any nearer to solving the crime?

'What a tragedy,' said Esther Moreno, whose husband was a Jewish banker. 'I read about it in the Jewish newspaper, *La Epoca.*'

Sylvia Jennings, whose husband was an eminent doctor, said it was likely that the police were looking into the new science of fingerprint identification, which might solve the crime.

'Do you think the police have any suspects?' Anoush Grigoryan asked. 'Surely it can't be that difficult. It had to be someone at the wedding.'

'Yes,' replied Sylvia, 'but if everyone has an alibi...'

They were all throwing around ideas, hoping Theodosia would shed some light on the situation, but she told them she knew as much as they did, which was not altogether true because there had been no mention of the type of gun used in the newspapers. The women thought she knew more than she was letting on but were too polite to question her more.

'Maybe someone has cast the evil eye on them,' said Dimitra, one of the handful of Greek members of the group. Everyone looked at her. They were educated women and were surprised she said such a thing. Her cheeks reddened.

'You don't still believe in that, do you?' Sylvia said. 'It's superstition.'

Dimitra was annoyed that a foreigner would question her. 'You never know. It does happen. I've seen it many times.'

'Aman!' laughed Sylvia.

The subject turned to Hamid. Hümeyra, one of the wives of Mustafa Bey, who was one of the sultan's military personnel, said she'd heard Hamid was a great womanizer. 'I knew of someone who'd had an affair with him, but when she found he was seeing other women too, she dropped him.'

There was a lot of tutting and deep sighs. 'There's so much gossip, no one knows what to believe any more,' someone else said.

Hümeyra looked offended. 'That's not gossip. His whole family are aware of his vices. He loved women and spent his father's money as if it flowed like water from the melting snows in the springtime.

What kind of woman wants that? If you ask me, Behice, goodness itself, is better off without him.'

'Like father, like son,' Anoush added. 'Didn't his father have the same reputation before Hateme tamed him?'

Theodosia was relieved when Maria brought in the food and the subject was dropped. Soon they were tucking into boreks, dolmas, and dips, and the conversation changed from murder to recipes and where they were going for summer holidays. One was going to Paris, Sylvia was going back to London for a few months, and Hümeyra was going to be home in Büyükada. Their appetites satisfied, the women packed up their embroidery, thanked Theodosia for a good day, and departed. As far as the murder was concerned, their curiosity remained unabated, but they would not press their good friend any more except to say that the next time they met they hoped the murder had been solved.

CHAPTER 10

THREE DAYS LATER, Chief Inspector Ibrahim sat in the same chair again, enjoying more delicious sweets made by Maria. He wore the same suit as last time and carried the same notebook, although Theodosia thought it looked much thicker. Next to him was another policeman who was introduced as Selahattin Bey. Selahattin worked with the inspector on important murder cases. He also requested that Abdul be in the meeting too as he was the one who had seen everything.

'What is the purpose of your visit today, Inspector?' Theodosia asked. 'I presume you must have discovered something or you wouldn't be here.'

He produced a piece of paper from his ever-growing file and proceeded to tell her that they had the guest list from the two days when Hamid had dinner and stayed with his female companion at the Pera Palace. One of the names made her gasp. It was the Grand Duchess Irena.

Reeling from the shock, she turned to the inspector, thinking he must have got the murder investigation mixed up with something entirely innocent. 'Is this all you have – a list? That doesn't prove they were together.'

He sighed. 'The truth is sometimes hard to deal with, Madame Theodosia. She often stayed there – with other men too – but on both these occasions she was accompanied by Hamid, son of Ferid Pasha. Selahattin Bey was the one who made inquiries. He has "contacts" there.' He turned to Selahattin and told him to tell her what he found out.

'They dined together in the restaurant, and although they booked separate rooms, they slept in the same bed. On both days, Hamid's bed was unmade: the chambermaid confirmed this, and she also confirmed the Grand Duchess's room showed signs of – how can I put it delicately – a night of intense, adventurous love-making!'

'Goodness.' Theodosia's hand went to her chest in shock. She knew Irena had lovers, but Hamid of all people! This news was even more shocking because she was well aware he was to be married and was even invited to the wedding.

Selahattin Bey, being the gentleman that he was, poured her a glass of water and handed it to her. She was so upset, she nearly dropped it.

'Now,' continued Inspector Ibrahim, 'you might recall a little more clearly who lives on Büyükada.'

'The Grand Duchess has a holiday home there.'

'That's right, and it was she who was picked up by Hamid. That too was confirmed when we showed photographs to a few people who work on the ferries.'

Theodosia looked at Abdul for some sort of explanation. 'Grand Duchess Irena of all people! She's been here – in this very house. Why didn't you recognise her?'

Abdul, back erect and hands on his knees as usual, reiterated what he'd said before. 'Her face was covered and when she got into the carriage, the curtains were drawn. It was as if she purposely didn't want anyone to recognise her.'

'Have you spoken to her?' Theodosia asked the inspector.

'I have. I paid her a visit at her home on the island. When faced with the fact that she'd had an intimate relationship with Hamid, she didn't deny it.'

'That doesn't mean that she murdered him though, and I thought you'd already spoken to her on the day of the murder.'

'We did and she confirmed she was in the house at the time, but didn't say anything about their relationship as she thought it wasn't important. In fact, when the subject of their relationship was brought up, she was quite open with us, even going as far as to say they'd struck up a relationship before he went to Paris and she met him when she was on holiday there. That was about a year ago.'

Still trying to absorb it all, Theodosia said the Grand Duchess usually liked men of her own age or older. Hamid was much younger than her.

The inspector smiled. 'She said she was flattered that a younger man would pursue her as he did. He gave her luxurious gifts – a gold necklace and earrings, and other trinkets. She laughed at the suggestion that she could have been jealous enough to kill him because, much as she enjoyed his company, she'd had better lovers.'

'She actually told you that!' Theodosia couldn't believe it.

'Her exact words were, "He was a wonderful man, funny and witty, a good lover, but not the best. I was happy he was getting married to Behice, but I knew his character well enough to presume that he would wander into the arms of another woman at the drop of a hat. So, Inspector, I had no need to murder him."'

'No motive then?'

'It appears not.'

'What about the gun? Did you show her a picture of the type used?'

'I did. She said she had a similar one which she often kept in her handbag. She showed me. It was indeed similar and we took it for examination, but it wasn't the one used on the day. It has since been returned to her.'

Theodosia breathed a sigh of relief. 'Then it wasn't Irene?'

'It seems not, but at the moment I do not rule anything out.' Inspector Ibrahim refilled his pipe while she and Abdul digested the information. 'People can be most imaginative when it comes to murder, you know.'

Theodosia looked at Abdul. 'I can't believe it – Irena and Hamid.'

After the inspector had allowed her time to digest this latest shock, he said he wanted to ask Abdul more about the French painter. 'The last time I was here, you told us about Hamid and the orange seller. Did you ever see the painter there with him? After all, the man did paint her.'

'Yes. There were a couple of times the two were together.'

'How did you view the Frenchman's attitude to her?'

'It was hard to tell. I was still trying to keep my distance in case they thought I was following them.'

'Would you say he was attracted to her?'

Abdul tried hard to think. 'I'm sorry, I really can't say.'

Theodosia turned to the inspector. 'Have you spoken with Monsieur Maurin again?'

'We went to the house. Ferid Pasha was not there and the maid said we were too late. The Frenchman had packed his bags and left about two hours earlier. "He is going back to Paris tonight," she said. Luckily, we caught him at Sirkeci Station just as he was about to board the Orient Express. He did not take kindly to being told he could not leave the country until he had answered more questions. "I answered all your questions before. There is no reason to stay here any longer. My friend is dead," he told us. He was extremely agitated.'

'That sounds highly suspicious, wouldn't you agree?' Theodosia said.

The inspector shrugged his shoulders. 'I cannot say whether he had a guilty conscience or was angry at the thought of wasting money on a first class ticket. The point is, no one is to leave Istanbul until the murder is solved. No one of interest to the investigation anyway.'

When he'd finished, he thanked them for their time, especially Abdul. 'Your manservant has uncovered more than you realise, Madame Theodosia. We will be in touch in a few days.'

Theodosia saw them off and then went back into the morning room where Abdul was still waiting. 'My God, I need a strong drink after that,' she said.

He poured her a brandy. 'This time I think I will partake in a little raki,' Abdul said, with a grave face. 'Allah forgive me.'

Theodosia smiled. 'God sees all and I'm sure he won't begrudge you a little raki after what we've just been told.' She took a long sip and shook her head, thinking about what they'd heard. 'Well, well! Grand Duchess Irena and Hamid: who would have guessed? Anyway, I now feel better that our snooping is paying off, even if we missed that one. I have a feeling the inspector will solve this murder soon.'

Abdul agreed and gave a rare smile. His mustache, blackened with boot polish, curled up at the end, looked even larger than usual. 'I might just have another raki, Madame Theodosia,' he said – just to clear my mind, of course.'

Theodosia laughed. 'Of course.' She pushed the bottle towards him. 'Help yourself. In fact you can take the bottle with you. You deserve it.'

Maria was in the kitchen preparing spices, meat, and nuts for a pilav when he walked by. She noticed something different about him and then spied the bottle of raki, which he was attempting to hide from her.

'I thought you didn't drink?' she said, in her nosy way.

The earlier, brief smile disappeared and he reverted back to his normal self. He gave her a dark look and shook his fist. 'Mind your own business and go back to your beans and peas,' he said in Turkish before switching to Greek. 'Yesterday you did not put enough pekmez in the food. The kyria will hire another cook if you are not careful.'

'Ah, the pekmez again! I will drown you in pekmez. *Eísai trelós,*' she called after him in Greek, waving her finger in a circle and then tapping the side of her head. 'You are crazy.'

Theodosia made another entry in her diary that evening. *My dearest Alexander, your friend and colleague, Chief Inspector Ibrahim, called at the house and gave me some shocking news. Grand Duchess Irena and Hamid have been lovers. As you can imagine, it came as a complete surprise. Irena is a beautiful woman and attracts the attention of many men, but she is at least ten years older than Hamid.*

I have a feeling that the inspector is closing in on the case. He is quite matter-of-fact when discussing the murder and shows little emotion, yet carefully studies others. He reminds me of a man who plays blackjack but won't declare his hand until he is sure he's won.

I recall that some of your cases had the most surprising outcome and I am rather fearful that when the murderer is finally revealed, I might know him – or her.

*

A full two weeks passed before she heard from the inspector again. This time, she went alone to attend a briefing at the police headquarters. Thanks to Abdul's information, a few more details had come to light. Theodosia listened carefully, making mental notes of everything he said.

'So you think you have solved the case then?' Theodosia asked.

'I have uncovered much more and I believe so, but I have a favour to ask of you first.'

'Whatever I can do to help, Inspector. I am at your service.'

They spent the next ten minutes discussing what it was he wanted her to do. Theodosia was perplexed, but she agreed.

'Thank you. I am going to ask Ferid Pasha for a meeting at his yali in Üsküdar in a week's time. I would appreciate it if you and Abdul would attend.'

'There is something else. In light of Behice Hanim's sudden illness, I had people check the food for poisoning.' The inspector looked uncomfortable when he made the next statement, as he was aware her cook had been there that day.

Theodosia immediately thought of the story of Zeynep and the poisoned dessert. Her heart skipped a beat as Maria had been extremely nervous. 'We found bottles of poisons in the store cupboard, but...'

'But what? Don't tell me there was poisoning involved too?'

'It seems not. All the food was fine, but was going off due to the heat, nothing else. We always look for signs of poison, which has been used as a weapon since time immemorial. Our early ancestors dipped their spearheads in snake venom and Socrates died by hemlock, and as you know, even some of our great sultans were poisoned. Many households store lethal substances that, when used in small doses for medicinal purposes – by people who know what they are doing, I must stress –can be beneficial. Most households keep poisons in one form or another to kill vermin, etcetera. Hateme Hanim told me that she keeps the key to the cupboard in the storeroom where they are kept and no one used it for a few days before the wedding. So we have ruled out Behice's illness as having anything to do with poison.'

'Did you really suspect someone had tried to kill them both – one way or another?'

'I told you. I don't rule anything out.'

Theodosia was greatly relieved that the incident of Zeynep and Maria had not raised its ugly head.

'I would like you to keep this conversation between ourselves,' the inspector continued. 'We don't want to attract any gossip that will find its way into the newspapers, do we?'

'I give you my word,' Theodosia said.

Abdul Agha was waiting for her when she left. The whole way back to the house, Theodosia thought about the meeting with the inspector. As she stepped down from the carriage, she turned to Abdul. 'I don't know about you, but I fear that there is something missing in what the inspector has just told me. I think he suspects more than he is letting on. He has asked me to do something for him. I might need your help again.'

'Aman! More spying, Madame Theodosia?' Abdul asked.

'Not exactly: just something to follow up on. Will you help me?'

He wondered what she was going to ask him to do this time and feared he might cross the line and get them both into trouble.

'Come and join me this evening. We'll talk about it then.'

Theodosia went into the house where the music of a Chopin sonata was coming from the drawing room. Electra was back to her studies playing the piano. Signore Salvatini was standing close by with his hands clasped behind his back, his face tilted upwards, and his eyes closed. When Electra stopped playing to greet her mother, her presence took him by surprise.

'Mademoiselle is improving in leaps and bounds,' he said enthusiastically. 'Soon you will see her performing on the stage. She will be the delight of all Constantinople.'

'It's all thanks to you, signore.' The Italian was used to compliments and Theodosia was only too happy to praise him. After all, she had spent a small fortune for the classes, but at least Electra's hard work was bearing fruit. 'Don't let me interrupt. I have things to do.'

Signore Salvatini bowed and Electra picked up from where she left off. In the meantime Theodosia went to the kitchen to discuss meals and food supplies with Maria. She decided not to tell her about her meeting until the murder was solved.

Afterwards, she went to the drawing room to search for one of Alexander's notebooks. After his death, she kept them all but he had so many it was hard to know where to look. She needed one in particular if she was going to help the inspector. Eventually she found it and after leafing through the pages was happy to see it contained just the information she was looking for. She put it aside, intending to discuss it later with Abdul Agha.

By now, Maria was used to Abdul's evening chats behind closed doors and constantly kept an eye out but, frustratingly, she had no idea what was going on. It didn't stop her snooping to listen at the door when she thought no one was looking, until one evening, Calliope caught her. She pulled her inside the kitchen and gave her a good telling off. 'If Kyria Theodosia finds out, you will be in trouble. If she wants you to know something, she will tell you. Do you see me listening behind doors? You are in a good household, Maria; don't forget that.' As she walked out of the room, she turned towards her, wagging her finger at her as a warning.

Maria was infuriated and started to swear in Greek under her breath. It was as if everyone else in the house knew what was going on except her.

Alone in the drawing room, Theodosia opened her diary and read through the last few week's writing. She had never envisioned writing down such thoughts, but there it was: a murder, so far unsolved.

My dearest Alexander, today I visited your friend Inspector Ibrahim and he has asked me to do something for him. I am going to look at some of your old casebooks. I think they will help us. Let us pray for a final outcome as we are all weary of this terrible tragedy. Give me your strength, my beloved. Yours always, Theodosia.

The following day, after finding out the information she was looking for in Alexander's notebook, Theodosia and Abdul set out on what they hoped would be one final mission to help solve the murder.

CHAPTER 11

THE DAY ARRIVED when Theodosia was summoned to the meeting at Ferid Pasha's waterside mansion. While she waited for Maria to bring out the breakfast on the terrace, she took the opportunity to wander through the garden to cut a few sweet-smelling roses to give to Calliope to be placed in her bedroom. It was another perfect summer's day, and the garden with its panoramic view calmed her, particularly in light of the impending meeting which she knew would be an ordeal. When Maria appeared, she informed her about the meeting. Maria burst into tears at the memory of that fateful day. In view of Maria's response, Theodosia decided not to tell her that the inspector had been looking into poisoning too.

'Have they found the murderer?' Maria asked.

'I don't know. Chief Inspector Ibrahim wants to go over a few things before the newspaper reporters start to speculate on the murder. You have not been asked to go, so that is a blessing for you.'

Maria crossed herself. 'Thank God. The questioning was so stressful for me. I don't think I would cope if I had to be questioned a second time. Who else is going? Have *all* the guests been asked too?'

'I can't tell you who will be there. I only know it has to be important or Inspector Ibrahim wouldn't put us through this. Goodness knows, it was bad enough when it happened. Let's hope it will soon be over and we can get on with our lives as before.'

Maria stood with her hands twisting her apron, looking miserable. '*Hayde*, Maria,' Theodosia said. 'Snap out of it. Get on with your work and don't fret.'

'I will pray for you, Kyria Theodosia,' Maria said.

Theodosia paid particular attention to what she wore that day. Her ensemble needed to suit the occasion, and it was sure to be solemn. After consultation with Calliope, she decided on a navy suit with a simple skirt and fitted jacket. To liven it up, she wore an ivory blouse embellished with lace at the front and on the cuffs of the sleeves. Her hat was a paler shade of blue with an enormous brim and decorated with ostrich feathers – some were the same ivory colour as the blouse and others were shades of blue ranging from cornflower to pale sky. Like Katerina, Theodosia was always proud of her ostrich plume hats. The feathers were acquired by an eminent Sephardic family who imported them from the Sahara for trade across the Mediterranean. Feeling a little like Inspector Ibrahim, she carried one of her larger bags in which she put a notebook containing her research, a painted fan, and a bottle of Jicky by Guerlain; it was one of the last presents Alexander gave her before his death. The fragrance – fresh, spicy, warm, and sensual –served as a reminder of him and his dedication to his short life's work. Wearing it she had the feeling he was with her, enveloping her in his strength. She would need it. It was going to be a long day.

Abdul waited outside with the carriage. Electra, who had not been asked to attend, stood next to Calliope and Maria and they waved goodbye. 'Good luck, Mama,' Electra shouted. Calliope put a reassuring arm around her.

They watched until the carriage disappeared through the gates before returning to the house. 'I wonder if all will be revealed today,' Electra said. 'Mama has tried to hide everything from me but I know this whole thing has taken its toll on her.'

'Your mother is a strong woman,' Calliope replied. 'Sooner or later we will find out.'

At the main docks, Abdul left the carriage and horses in the care of someone and they boarded a small barge to cross the water to the Asian side, reaching the private landing dock of Ferid Pasha's house in the early afternoon. Quite a few barges were already moored there and they were forced to moor further along the shoreline where the water was choppy, the waves rising and falling in the soft breeze. Two policemen helped Theodosia out of the boat and one accompanied them towards the house. Approaching the place again gave her goosebumps.

The bustle and excitement of Behice and Hamid's marriage had well and truly gone, replaced by the tranquility of the Garden of Enchantment, where the delightful humming of insects and bees and the chirping of birds filtered through the trees on the soft warm breeze from the water. Yet for all its quiet beauty, there was a sense of foreboding.

Where the orchestra had played on that fateful day, there were now two policemen and one of Ferid Pasha's guards. When they saw the three approach, one of them opened the door. The pasha's butler welcomed Abdul and Theodosia and showed them to the large sunroom where all the other guests were assembled. The room was enormous, filled with opulent furniture, both French and Ottoman, sofas and chairs decorated with the best rose and blue silk brocade from Bursa, and ornaments from around the world. Open French windows led to a terrace with ornate pots of orange and lemon trees, and beyond was the Bosphorus with a view of Constantinople's beautiful skyline of mosques and minarets. Theodosia recalled that it was in this room, with its grand piano which stood in one corner, now adorned with a crystal candelabra and photographs, that she first met Signore Salvatini when he gave a recital. Unlike now, that was a joyous occasion.

Trays of food had been placed on small side tables alongside the chairs and sofas, but no one seemed to be in the mood to eat.

Ferid Pasha, the Grand Imam of Istanbul, Inspector Ibrahim, and Selahattin Bey greeted her, their faces showing the gravity of the meeting. Theodosia had not expected Bidar and her daughter to be there, but just to keep his eye on things, the sultan had sent two important officials from the palace to report back on the proceedings. The atmosphere was sombre and heavy with expectation. No one knew what to expect and a cloud of despair hung over everyone. One glance around the room showed that there were about twenty people there, most of whom she knew. She acknowledged them as she and Abdul made their way to a sofa large enough to sit four people. Next to her, in a high-backed armchair, was Hateme, who kept wiping the tears from her eyes with a white monogrammed handkerchief. She looked gaunt with grief and seemed to have aged considerably in the last few weeks.

Theodosia knew it would be a mixed gathering. Ömer and Hafsa were there with Behice and Ayşe. Hafsa was clasping Behice's hand, occasionally stroking it as if she were calming a small child, while Ayşe sat on the other side of her mother with her back erect and her face somewhat cold and detached, staring ahead across the blue waters towards the Dolmabahçe Palace. Sitting on a wooden stool behind them was Behice's personal maid. Seated in the centre of the room were the Grand Duchess Irena and Katerina. Out of respect, they too had dressed suitably for the occasion, their bright silks replaced by darker tones and an absence of jewellery. To their right was the artist, Pierre, his face clearly showing his displeasure at being prevented from returning to Paris, and next to him were two people who Theodosia had never seen before. But one of them she instantly recognized from the painting. It was the orange seller.

Pierre had certainly captured her beauty in his painting, but in real life, she was one of the most beautiful women Theodosia had ever seen. Her beauty was so striking she even outshone Katerina and the Grand Duchess. The girl wore a simple cotton turquoise dress with a gold sash and yellow slippers. Her long black tresses tumbled freely over her shoulders, almost reaching her waist, and while all the other women in the room wore hats, she wore a colourful silk scarf wrapped around her head in a band, tied on the right and allowed to drape freely through her tresses. She had an almond-shaped face with a pale olive complexion, and her amber coloured eyes were bewitching, almost hypnotic. But it was her lips that Theodosia noticed the most. Small and sensuous, and as pink as rose petals, they were the kind of lips that suggested the promise of sweetness and passion to those who kissed them. She was certainly not from the upper echelons of society, yet she lit up the room without the need of fine fashions, or fancy hats and hairdos. Hers was a real beauty and it seemed to Theodosia that she had no idea just how beautiful she was. There was a naivety to her.

Next to her was a thick-set, middle-aged man wearing the clothes of an Anatolian merchant – baggy pants and boots, a simple white shirt and a red cummerbund – who appeared most uncomfortable in the company of men in fine suits. Theodosia surmised he was a relative or friend, possibly even her father.

The last guest to enter the room was Hamid's personal valet, who also drove his carriage when Hamid lived in his family's city home on his return from Paris.

Ferid Pasha closed the door and went over towards his wife. He stood behind her and put a steadying, affectionate hand on her shoulder. She in turn momentarily tilted her head and lay her cheek on his hand. Theodosia was touched by his tenderness.

Inspector Ibrahim and the Grand Imam moved into the centre of the room and the inspector stood with his hands behind his back while the imam opened the Koran, ready to say prayers.

'I open this meeting in the name of Allah, the most merciful, the most compassionate. Let us now offer a prayer for Hamid, whose earthly body rests in the Valley of the Silent Ones, but whose soul has ascended to heaven and now walks in the path of righteousness. He was a beloved son, friend, and' – his eyes moved to Behice – 'husband: a man taken too early from us.' The imam turned to a page in the Koran and began to recite a prayer. There were a few mumbles as several people joined in. He finished with another verse from the Koran. 'Truly we belong to Allah and to him we shall return.' He bowed and walked away, taking a seat next to the sultan's officials, leaving Inspector Ibrahim alone in the middle of the room and the mood even gloomier than before.

Inspector Ibrahim carefully scanned everyone's faces in the room to make sure he had their full attention before telling them why they were there. He was not a man to mince words and neither did he want to string this case out any longer out of respect for the bereaved.

'Thank you all for coming today. I called this meeting because in my opinion, we are close to solving Hamid's death. Such a callous murder will not go unpunished. In fact, I will go as far as to say, the murderer is possibly sitting amongst us now.'

There were loud gasps as everyone glanced around with suspicion. At these words, Hateme let out a long wail and vigorously fanned herself. But the strain was already too much and she began to faint until she was quickly brought around by Selahattin Bey, who held a bottle of smelling salts to her nose. She sat in her oversized chair like a rag doll and the only thing stopping her from falling was her husband's firm grip on her shoulder. Inspector Ibrahim waited patiently until she was fully recovered, even asking if she would like to sit outside on the terrace, but she refused. In an authoritarian voice, he asked for silence. Eyes still darted around the room, hoping to catch a glimpse of someone with a suspicious look or nervous twitch of guilt, but at least everyone quietened down.

He continued. 'I know this is a shock to most of you, and if you will bear with me, I will proceed.' He paused for a moment as if wondering where best to start.

'When the son of such a powerful figure of the empire is murdered, and on such a day of happiness too, my colleague Selahattin Bey and myself knew this had to have been premeditated. Few would risk committing such a crime in a situation where they could have been discovered so quickly. Usually, a murder takes place in a location where the murderer can leave the scene of the crime undetected. That was not the case here. Ferid Pasha's house was well secured. This leads us to one conclusion only: that the murderer knew the house well. He – or she – knew that a wedding was taking place.'

At the mention of a possible "she", everyone looked aghast and began glancing at all the women in the room. Surely it was not possible a woman had committed this murder.

'After we conducted our interviews that fateful day, we took a closer look at everyone as there were lots of unanswered questions. Too many, in fact, and if I might be so bold as to say so, a few people's stories or uneasy body language made us embark on a trail of further enquiries. Naturally, many were ruled out straight away as they were nowhere near the scene of the crime when it took place.' He scrutinized their faces. 'What is unimportant to the average person is most important to the police. We looked through our files again and did a little digging around. It is amazing what lurks under a heavy stone. Moving stones is what we do. Some stones yield diamonds.'

Theodosia could see that those in the room were perplexed as to where all this was leading, but she also sensed the inspector knew this too. It was all part of an act. Maybe someone would become frightened and blurt something out. Alexander told her people often did that when they were under close examination. The strain was unbearable.

'It is all about motive,' he said as he slowly started to pace the room. '*Who* had a motive for wanting Hamid dead? *Who* would benefit by his death?' He walked around the room looking everyone in the eyes again, this time standing closer to them, even Theodosia. The fear in the room was palpable. No one wanted to think of themselves as being associated with a murderer.

'All murderers leave a trail,' he said. 'It's a matter of uncovering it – of locating the right stone that conceals the diamond .He who seeks answers will find them.'

At this point, Ferid Pasha spoke out. 'Inshallah, Inspector Ibrahim, but please get to the point. Can't you see my good wife is suffering? We are *all* suffering.'

The inspector stood and faced him. 'Ah, Ferid Pasha, that is where you are wrong. Not everyone in this room is suffering.' There was a pause. 'As you have been the first to speak up, perhaps it is only right that I begin with your good self.'

Ferid Pasha was accustomed to being regarded as a figure of authority. Now his face displayed shock and indignation. He was about to speak when Inspector Ibrahim put his hand out to stop him.

'Let us take a look at your relationship with your son, Hamid, if we may. It was not a good one, was it?'

Ferid, a man of words, was at a loss at what to say.

'Do you deny that your relationship with him was not a good one?'

'I am like any father. We had our moments, but he was a good son.'

The inspector studied him for a few moments. 'Tell me, Ferid Pasha, is it true that you brought your son back from Paris because he did not live up to your expectations; that he did not study as you'd hoped and that he lived the reckless life of a spendthrift, a gambler, and a womanizer?'

Ferid's cheeks reddened and his face looked like thunder. Others in the room also looked shocked.

'Unfortunately, that is true. I wanted to put a stop to his behavior.'

'And you thought you would do that by marrying him off to your friend's youngest daughter, who, by all accounts is of a quiet, shy character, and in all probability would defend the family's good name should he choose to misbehave again.'

Ferid grudgingly agreed. 'I thought marriage would be good for him.'

The inspector turned to Ömer Pasha. 'And you, Ömer Pasha, were you aware of the reason Hamid was brought back to Constantinople?'

The way Hafsa looked at her husband told Theodosia that her friend did not know as much as Theodosia had thought. Why had he kept all this from his wife?

'I knew Hamid was rather an impetuous man, yes, but I also felt as his father did, that back in Istanbul, he would change, especially after he married and had a family of his own.' He glanced at Behice, who stared ahead with an expressionless face as if she had detached herself from the conversation. 'I love my daughter and wanted the best for her. Ferid has been a good friend. He is a loyal man to his majesty the sultan and the empire.'

'Did you not question why he desired Hamid to marry and not his elder son from his first marriage who, like his father, has a good position in the military: a position with excellent prospects?'

'I am aware of his other son – a good man – but it was Hamid that Ferid wished Behice to marry.'

The inspector caught them all off guard with his next statement. 'And were you aware that on his return from Paris, Hamid embezzled many thousands of liras from his father.'

The room went so quiet you could hear a pin drop. Hafsa looked at him, utterly speechless.

Ömer turned to look at his friend, his lips pinched tightly and his eyes burning with anger. 'No! I certainly was not aware!'

All eyes now settled on Ferid. In that moment, he appeared small in stature and importance and Theodosia noticed, for the first time, silver streaks at the sides of his jet back hair.

'Perhaps you could enlighten us on this situation, Pasham. I believe you discovered this fact around the time you approached Ömer Pasha and his good wife with the marriage proposal.'

'I found out when I went to the bank. Seeing that our funds were very much lower than usual, I sought out the manager. That's when I knew my signature had been forged. When I confronted my son, he said he owed thousands of liras from gambling and if he didn't pay it back, the family and our good name would be ruined. He even threatened to kill himself.'

At hearing this, Hateme, who until now, had been sitting in a daze, dabbing her eyes, stood up and turned angrily to him. 'May Allah protect you! Ever since I became your wife, I have given you my endless love.' She slapped him across his face with her fan. 'Our family has served the sultan for generations. You could not have hurt me more than if you had pieced my heart with a dagger. How could you let this happen?'

Her actions and words took everyone by surprise. Ferid took a step closer to hold her but she moved away. 'Get away from me.'

The emotion was such that her legs started to give way and she started to feel faint again. Selahattin Bey and another man rushed over and caught her and took her out on to the terrace to get some fresh air.

'I kept it from you because I knew you wouldn't understand,' Ferid shouted out as the men carried her outside. 'If this is anyone's fault it is *yours*. You spoilt him all his life – pandered to his every whim. He could do no wrong in your eyes.' He realized it was unbecoming behaviour and covered his face in despair.

Theodosia thought it an embarrassing moment for all in the room. She had never seen either of them act this way. It made her wonder if Alexander ever kept secrets from her for fear of upsetting her. She doubted it, but human nature being what it was... She would never know now.

Inspector Ibrahim put his hands out to calm the situation. 'This is not helpful,' he said, matter-of-factly. 'The point is, Ferid Pasha, you *did* have a motive to kill your son, didn't you? And you *were* in the house at the time.'

'If you put it that way, yes, I did. I was angry with him, but I was not the one who killed him – my own flesh and blood. I loved him, despite what he'd become.'

'Thank you, Pasham.'

Theodosia caught the inspector's eye. What had just taken place was devastating, but it had to be brought out into the open. It was Hateme she felt sorry for. A mother's love knows no bounds and she would not take this insult lightly. In all probability, they would divorce after this. No wonder Ferid kept had kept his son's behaviour quiet.

CHAPTER 12

AT THIS POINT Inspector Ibrahim told everyone he wanted to confer with Selahattin Bey. The butler, who had been standing outside the room listening to what was going on, tried to ease the situation by asking the maids to quickly send in refreshments. Three nervous young women entered, passing around trays of tea and sherbets while everyone in the room tried desperately to put on a brave face in front of one another.

Ten minutes later the inspector resumed the meeting. This time he focused his attention on Hafsa. Ömer protested, asking him to leave his wife out of this. 'I already told you that I did not tell my wife of Ferid's problems with his son. Can't you see her heart is bleeding? Have mercy.'

Hafsa touched his hand to quieten him. 'I have nothing to hide. Let the inspector ask whatever he wants. He is only doing his job.'

'Thank you, Hanimefendi,' Ibrahim said. 'I am sorry that you were not aware of all the details, misguided as it was, and I can only hope that your husband did indeed try to protect you because it seems evident that he has deep feelings for you.' He gave a heavy sigh. 'Unfortunately, human beings do not always behave as we expect them to. If they did, well – my job would be much easier.'

Theodosia could tell he was trying to steady Hafsa's nerves.

'Is it true that you asked your husband why he chose Behice to be married, rather than Ayşe Hanim, your older daughter?'

Hafsa looked surprised. 'It is. Where did you get this information?'

'I am not at liberty to say, except that our investigations are thorough.'

Theodosia felt most uncomfortable. The last thing she wanted to do was hurt her good friend. She desperately hoped Hafsa wouldn't blame her, but she had only done what she thought was best.

'Is it also true that Ayşe expressed, on more than one occasion, that she had feelings for Hamid?'

'That's correct, although I didn't realise that until after the marriage was arranged.'

'You were angry about this, were you not?'

'My husband and I exchanged heated words about it, yes. Ayşe was extremely upset. She told me she felt betrayed.'

The inspector looked at Ömer. 'Pasham, why didn't you listen to your good wife?'

He took a deep breath. 'As I told you before, it was between my friend and I. We considered we knew what was best for our family.' He searched for the right words. 'Women tend to get emotional about these things, particularly when it comes to their children. Sometimes these emotions cloud their judgment and they fail to see the bigger picture...' His voice trailed off in embarrassment.

Hafsa turned and looked at him, her face full of indignation. 'I tried to reason with you but you refused to listen. I fell in love with a lion, yet a sheep took his place. Your pride made you deaf to your conscience.'

Ömer lowered his head in shame, just as Ferid had. Neither wife had ever dared to say such things in public before.

Hafsa's look of disapproval unnerved him. 'Hafsa, my beloved, I beseech you from the bottom of my heart, please forgive me. I thought that what I did was for the best.' His hands reached out to hold her shoulders in an effort to placate her, but she shook herself free. Through her tears she told him that this was not the time and place to argue.

'Please, Hanimefendi; calm yourself,' Inspector Ibrahim said. 'Crying won't help.'

Confronting people like this was never easy for him, no matter how many times he did it.

He turned his attention to Ayşe. 'My good lady, can you tell me if it is true that you had feelings for Hamid?'

Her lips narrowed as she tried hopelessly to hide her rage. 'I was upset that it was my sister who my father chose.'

The inspector spun around to face Ferid. 'I would like to ask if Hamid chose Behice of his own free will, or did you?'

'I did. On reflection, I should have asked him, but I knew Behice was Ömer's favourite daughter. He called her his angel and he spoilt her just as my wife spoilt Hamid.'

Ayşe looked even angrier when she heard this.

'Ayşe Hanim, your displeasure is evident,' the inspector said. He came straight to the point. 'In my opinion, you had the perfect motive to kill Hamid.'

The group gasped aloud. Was he actually accusing her?

Ayşe's voice was clear and determined. 'I hated my father for choosing my sister, and I hated my mother for going along with it. I know my sister. She may be pretty, but she was not right for him. I loved Hamid and he knew it. You said before that he was a womanizer, but he declared he had feelings for me before he went to Paris and I told him I would wait. So you see, it should have been me, not her. Yes, I hated them.' She was trembling with anger.

Theodosia felt sorry for her. Clearly she did not know the type of man Hamid was.

The inspector gave her a moment to collect herself. 'You were in the house at the time of the murder. Where were you?'

Ayşe threw her hands in the air. 'I can't recall exactly.'

'Try to think?'

'I *am* thinking. It is most likely I was in the bathroom.'

'Did anyone see you?'

'I don't know. There were people everywhere in the house – looking at gifts, talking to others.'

'I put it to you again, Ayşe Hanim, that you had a strong motive to kill Hamid. If you couldn't have him, you made sure your sister wouldn't. That's correct, isn't it?'

Ayşe jumped out of her chair as the words tumbled out of her mouth. 'I could *never* kill the man I love. Never! I swear on the holy Koran, *I* am not the murderer.' She sat down again and, in a quieter tone, said she was shattered by his death.

The feeling of anxiety in the pit of everyone's stomachs had steadily grown to a hard knot of tension. No one knew where it was all leading and Theodosia could tell the growing distrust was tearing everyone apart.

Inspector Ibrahim clasped his hands behind his back. He addressed everyone in the room. 'This is a murder investigation and as such, every question, however intrusive, is pertinent, and at the moment, all cards are on the table.'

Next, Inspector Ibrahim turned his attention to Katerina. 'Katerina Hanim, is it true that you were aware of the deceased's fondness for women?'

There was a pause while she considered what to say, but she could not lie. 'That's correct.'

'How did you know?'

'It was common knowledge. He had lots of mistresses.'

The inspector nodded his head a little. 'Common knowledge to some, but not to others apparently.' Katerina looked at Ayşe, feeling sorry the poor girl had been deceived. 'Were you also aware that he had been having an affair with your friend, the Grand Duchess Irena?'

The group looked at one another again. Most of them knew Irena to be a flirt, but to have an affair with a man much younger than herself? That seemed unthinkable.

Ayşe shot the Grand Duchess an angry glance. 'That can't be true.'

'Ayşe Hanim,' the inspector said, trying to conceal his irritation at her outbursts, 'if you cannot contain yourself, I will have to ask you to go to a separate room where you will be looked after by a policeman until this investigation is over.' He turned back to Katerina. 'Please answer my question.'

'I was aware she met him on a trip to Paris, but I thought nothing of it. They are good friends.'

Inspector Ibrahim turned to the Grand Duchess, who sat calmly fanning herself. She had deliberately toned down her fashionable attire to suit the sombre occasion yet still looked as elegant and attractive as ever. 'Can you enlighten us on your relationship with Hamid? Was he just a "friend"?'

'I've known him since he was a young boy.'

'When did you start having a relationship with him?' Everyone in the room was staring at her with more than a hint of curiosity.

The Grand Duchess sighed. 'A relationship? What exactly do you mean?'

'I think you know full well what I mean. Do you want me to spell it out? You were having an affair, were you not?'

Irena continued fanning herself to keep her composure. 'We met up occasionally, that's all. It wasn't exactly what you would call a relationship.'

'Nevertheless, there *was* intimacy between you both, wasn't there?'

Irena held her head high. 'At times, yes. He pursued me.' Ferid gave her a dark look.

The inspector asked if Ferid knew about this.

'I certainly did not,' he replied, his voice shaking in anger.

The Grand Duchess gave a little half-smile. A smile that Theodosia knew hid something much deeper. She felt as if Ferid wanted to say more, but stopped himself. She realised that Irena knew he would be careful with his words because Ferid himself had pursued her on many occasions.

The inspector also noted Ferid's reaction to Irena's words. 'I am not here to judge how people conduct themselves in private; I am only here to solve a murder.' He walked over to stand more directly in front of the duchess. 'I interviewed you at length and you have a gun similar to the murder weapon. Is that so?'

There were murmurings in the group. 'That's right. I showed it to you and you agreed that it had not been recently fired.'

'Yes, that's true. Do you own any other pistols?'

'I have one at home in Saint Petersburg.'

'Did anyone else know you had this particular type of gun?'

'It's possible. Many ladies possess such a gun because it fits inside a small bag.'

'An ideal place to conceal a murder weapon?'

The Grand Duchess agreed, and like Theodosia had suggested to the inspector herself, stated that men could also conceal such a weapon in their coat jackets. She added that she had no reason to kill Hamid anyway. 'I was happy for him when he told me he had found someone he finally loved.'

'Is that so? Are we talking about the same woman?'

Irena looked confused. 'I presumed he meant Behice.'

'You mean to tell us that Hamid, a man who is, to put it mildly, flirtatious and enjoys the company of many women – the thrill of the chase and the conquest – had suddenly fallen head over heels in love? Didn't you think it strange; this sudden change in him?'

'Strange? No. Everyone can fall in love, even a man like Hamid. There is always someone who can sweep us off our feet. I've seen it time and time again.'

'And you thought that someone was Behice?'

The Grand Duchess thought for a few moments. 'I didn't have any reason to think otherwise. Behice is a beautiful, kind young woman. All I knew was that this time, I was sure he really had fallen in love. He seemed so happy.'

'What about her sister, Ayşe Hanim? Did he ever mention her?'

After what Ayşe had said, Irena seemed hesitant to speak. The inspector tapped his foot on the carpet patiently, waiting for her to answer.

'Only once.'

'What did he say about her?'

'That she was a lovely girl, but he was not interested in her – as a wife I mean.'

Ayşe's anger rose again. 'He would never say that about me! He said he cared.'

Inspector Ibrahim was losing his patience. 'Please, Ayşe Hanim, I know this is distressing, but you have been warned about causing a scene and it is my last warning.' Ayşe sat back in her chair sulking like a child, the tears rolling down her cheeks.

'Hush, child,' Hafsa said, patting her on the thigh. 'Please don't make it any worse. It is unbecoming.'

All this made Theodosia realize that she must be very sensitive with Electra as she was now becoming of age, and she resolved not to put her own interests above her daughter's.

CHAPTER 13

Inspector Ibrahim asked Selahattin Bey to hand him one of his many folders. He opened it and glanced through the pages before turning to the Grand Duchess again. 'What would you say if I told you the woman Hamid had lost his heart to was not Behice Hanim? That it was, in fact, this lady here with us today.' He extended his arm towards the orange seller.

A multitude of emotions from shock to anger showed on everyone's faces. Some even laughed whilst Hafsa covered her face with her hands. 'Allah have mercy on us.'

'Quiet, please,' Ibrahim called out sternly. 'Let us be civil.'

Theodosia and Abdul Agha glanced quickly at each other. She wondered if the inspector was going to reveal who had told him about Hamid's relationship with the orange seller.

The Grand Duchess studied the woman and smiled. 'Although she

141

is beautiful, I'm afraid that even Hamid would realise such a match would not be deemed suitable.'

The inspector clasped his hands behind his back. He was a good man and was used to such comments but in his heart he found the arrogance of these people quite overwhelming. 'May I remind you that Hurrem, who married the Great Suleiman the Magnificent, Allah rest his soul, and, who I would like add, is an ancestor of our current majesty, was once a slave. Anything is possible.'

At this, the dignitaries from the palace stopped writing their notes and took a good look at the woman in question. The Grand Duchess fanned herself even faster and the guests felt shame that they too had felt as Irena did.

'Of course we are all aware of this, Inspector. I did not mean to insult his majesty.'

'Nevertheless, what I say is true.' He looked at everyone in the room. 'Hamid lost his heart to this good lady.'

'Have mercy on us,' Hafsa said. 'Surely there is some mistake. How can you compare this... this orange seller with my beautiful Behice?'

'Hafsa Hanim, didn't we just establish that love knows no bounds?'

Hafsa struggled for words. 'It is an insult – an orange seller; probably illiterate too. Where is your proof?'

Inspector Ibrahim opened his file. 'It's all documented in here.' He tapped a page with his index finger on which he wore a decorative gold ring set with a large sapphire. He walked towards the orange seller and she looked down at the floor, her face flushed with embarrassment. The inspector reached out and held her chin up. 'Please tell us your name, Küçük Hanim?'

'Gizem,' the young lady replied.

'Mystery! Your name means mystery, and that is what you are to us.' He turned towards the man next to her. 'And you are her father, Mohammed?'

'Her adopted father, Efendim. The girl is an orphan.'

'Thank you.' Inspector Ibrahim picked up two books lying on a nearby coffee table: one in Turkish, the other in French.

'Can you read these?' he asked.

She glanced at them and shook her head. Clearly she was illiterate. He turned back to Hafsa. 'Your question has been answered.' Hafsa apologised for embarrassing her.

Theodosia felt sorry for them both. The situation was agonizing for everyone, and the longer it went on, the more tense it became.

'Now, Gizem, my dear lady, I don't want you to be afraid. What I want to know is...' Ibrahim paused for a moment to think, then began again. 'What I want you to tell us is how you came to know Hamid. In your own words, please.' To appear less intimidating, he pulled up a chair and sat next to her. Being at eye level was far less threatening.

Everyone's eyes were on the orange seller, who seemed so shy, she could barely speak. Hateme, who had recovered from her fainting episode, came back into the room to hear this too. Theodosia thought the poor girl looked like a small bird with a broken wing inside a room full of birds of Paradise.

What emerged was mostly what Abdul Agha and Theodosia had told the inspector, except that she was able to fill in the gaps – the conversations that Abdul was not able to overhear or what took place when they were behind closed doors. It was quite a revelation.

'I met Hamid one day when I was selling oranges in my usual spot outside the Bayezid Gate. I had noticed him passing before, but he hadn't noticed me. As you know, the area gets very crowded. One day, he came over to buy a couple of oranges. He said I was very pretty but I took no notice as men often make comments. Also, I could tell by the manner of his dress and speech that I was not of his class. It was a surprise when he came back the next day, and the day after. The third time he asked me if I would like to have tea with him. I asked him to stop, as passersby noticed his persistence, and refused him, saying that I had my oranges to sell. I know it's not much, but we depend on what little money I make. "Just tell me your name," he asked. He pleaded with me, telling me he was consumed by love.

'I asked if he would leave me alone if I told him and he said he would. "It's Gizem," I said, but he didn't stop. He asked where I lived and I told him he was embarrassing me. He then asked if I knew who he was. "I am not just any man," he said. "I am Hamid, son of Ferid Pasha." I jumped up and, in doing so, upset my orange stand. Bright orange balls of fruit scattered, rolled down the hill where street urchins gathered them up and ran off with them.

'"Now look what you've made me do," I said angrily. He took out his wallet and squeezed money into my hand. "I will pay for each one and more." It was more than I earned in a week.'

Gizem glanced up, her eyes scanning the people in the room as if she fully expected no one to understand her plight. Her gaze momentarily settled on Pierre. The exchange between them didn't go unnoticed by the inspector or Theodosia and Abdul.

'I didn't want to accept the money, but he insisted.'

'But you did give in, did you not, eventually?' Ibrahim's voice was calm and assuring, without being judgmental.

'Yes. I accepted it, because when I looked into his eyes there was something about him that made my heart stir.'

'Was your father there at the time?'

'No. My father helped carry the baskets of oranges in the morning and then went away. He always returned when it was time for me to go home.'

'What time was that?'

'It depended on the weather and whether the oranges were selling well. He knew there were other vendors still there even when the doors to the Grand Bazaar were closed.'

'So you finally gave in and accepted the invitation to go for a drink with Hamid, then. Was it the money that made you change your mind?' His words were soft but the question sounded a little harsh.

'Look around you, Efendim. Everyone here views me as a whore, but I am innocent.'

'I can assure you that no one will say such things, Hanim Kizim. Please continue.'

Gizem hesitated. 'No, it wasn't the money. I did like him, very much in fact, and he seemed genuine. It was just a glass of tea after all. A girlfriend who sits nearby and who sells dried apricots and figs whispered that she would look after my oranges while I was gone. "Go," she said. "Grab a little happiness from this miserable life. Your secret is safe with me."'

'Did your father know?'

'Not at first. I gave him the money and told him a man had been kind to me. He told me to be careful – a poor girl with a man I didn't know. He warned me not to bring shame on his good name.'

Theodosia looked at the girl's father, who sat proudly upright, his expression one of dignity despite his poverty. She glanced towards the sultan's administrators, who were busily taking notes.

Gizem went on to say that although Hamid kept saying he had fallen in love with her, she still couldn't bring herself to believe it. 'Then he started to write me love poems. On the days when he didn't come, he sent them with his manservant. They were the most beautiful words I'd ever heard.' She closed her eyes and her sweet lips smiled when she recalled them.

"The moment you left me, sweetness was stolen from my tongue.
I turned to wax, burned like a candle
all night, scorched by fire, no honey.
No way to reach you, no way to touch your beauty.
My body lies here in ruins.
My soul, a night owl."

Most people in the room recognised the poem as one by the Persian poet, Rumi, but Gizem thought they were Hamid's words.

Inspector Ibrahim asked her to point to the man on the other side of the room. 'Is this true?' he asked Hamid's manservant.

The man nodded, avoiding the angry gaze of Hateme and Ferid. 'It is, Efendi.'

Ibrahim opened the file. In it were several pieces of paper with short verses on them. 'For everyone here, could you please say if these were the poems Hamid sent you?'

She looked at them carefully. 'They are.'

'Küçük Hanim, you are illiterate. How did you know these were love poems?'

'I took them to the scribe and he read them out to me.'

'I see. Did you ask the scribe to write anything in return – something for you to give Hamid?'

'I do not possess his way with words, so I asked the scribe to compose something suitable.' There was a pause. The tears were rolling down Ayşe's cheek and Behice stared, stony-faced, at the girl. 'No one had ever treated me in that way before. My father is a good man, but all my life I felt worthless. Day in, day out, selling fruit at the market; that was my life until Hamid came along and gave me hope. He said he wanted to take me away from all this.'

'Is this the point where your relationship developed?' Ibrahim asked.

Gizem's face reddened. She looked at her father, waiting for his permission to continue. He nodded. By now, everyone had gone quiet. The room was filled with tension and expectation.

'He started to take me to a small hotel owned by a friend who he said would keep our relationship a secret.' She paused and took a deep breath. 'That's where... where I gave myself to him.' This time the gasps in the room were loud and longer. Gizem's face reddened, yet there was a flash of defiance in her eyes. She hated the way people looked at her. 'Think of me what you will, but I believed he loved me and still do.'

Ferid Pasha shook his head in despair. 'What sort of man did I raise?' he said aloud. 'My heart bleeds.'

Theodosia recalled the words "like father like son" as the inspector urged him to keep his thoughts to himself.

Feeling safe in the inspector's presence, with each sentence, Gizem became bolder. She looked at Ferid and with a bewitching smile – the same smile that had obviously turned Hamid's head – said, 'Efendim, your son did not force himself upon me. He made me feel alive. If anything, it is *you* who killed him even before he was murdered.' She stood up and pointed at him. 'He pleaded with you not to marry him off, but you wouldn't listen. When he told you he wanted to marry me, you hastened the marriage.'

Hateme looked at her with distaste and quietly mumbled to herself, 'Aman! Who can believe all this?'

Mohammed tugged at Gizem's skirt. She apologised and sat down, and the inspector handed her a glass of water.

'Were you aware that he was to betrothed to Behice Hanim?'

'Not at that point. Only that his family had chosen someone for him. He described her as a good woman, but he loved only me. He talked about us running away and showering me with gifts. I knew that was wrong and tried to discourage him, telling him he could not do that to his family, even though I felt they didn't understand him. I also knew that in time he would come to realize I was not for him and most likely resent me.'

People in the room looked at each other. Who was this curious girl who held such sway over Hamid? Theodosia sensed some even felt sorry for her.

Gizem put her head in her hands, the bangles on her wrists jangling playfully in the silence of the room. 'He said he would kill himself if he couldn't have me and then started to tell me the story of Romeo and Juliet. It made me cry. I did not want us to end up that way.'

'When did you find out it was Behice Hanim that he was to marry?' Inspector Ibrahim asked.

She looked at Pierre. 'He told me.'

'You mean Monsieur Maurin, the man who painted your portrait?'

'Yes.'

'Monsieur Maurin is from Paris. He speaks very little Turkish.'

'Efendim, I may not be able to read or write, but I do know quite a lot of French. Working at the Grand Bazaar, one learns to pick up languages quickly. My father taught me that from an early age.'

'Tell us what happened, Küçük Hanim.'

'Why don't you ask him – Monsieur Pierre? He will tell you.'

CHAPTER 14

PIERRE, WHO WAS still fuming over being there in the first place, had been trying hard to follow what the inspector was saying. When it was his turn, he did not hold back. The conversation reverted to French, the lingua franca of the upper classes in Constantinople, even though almost everyone in the room understood and spoke several languages fluently, including Greek, Armenian, English, German, and Italian. Several, like Ferid and Ömer Pasha, spoke Russian too, as did Grand Duchess Irena.

'I was invited to this fine city by my good friend, Hamid,' Pierre said. 'At the time he'd just received his father's letter ordering him back home and he was not aware that his father wished him to marry. He expected to return to Paris. This is my first time here, and as an artist, I've followed the works of many fine Orientalist painters in the east, so I was looking forward to it. When I was asked to stay with him, we expected to spend some weeks here and then travel around for a few months as I wanted to make sketches and paint your fascinating country. Such was my enthusiasm that I even took Turkish lessons so that I could get by, especially in the countryside.

'I arrived here about two weeks after Hamid. Naturally, I expected us to discuss our travel plans, but instead, I found him in a state of despair.'

'Why was that?' asked Ibrahim.

'He and his father had been arguing. The pasha told him he was angry with his idle ways in Paris and was going to cut off his money if he didn't marry, settle down, and take up a respectful position. I believe he wanted him to go to the Military Academy like his half-brother.'

'*Was* he an idle man in Paris, monsieur?'

Pierre looked rather sheepish, deliberating on what to say. It was hard to defend Hamid's lifestyle of women and gambling in Paris. 'Let's say that his temperament was not cut out for the military.'

'Please enlighten us?'

'He was a free spirit. His nature was rebellious.'

Inspector Ibrahim smiled. 'You seem to know your friend quite well. Did you spend a lot of time together in Paris?'

'Yes. He came to my studio and I painted his portrait very early during his stay there. We got talking and I realised he was somewhat of a lost soul and I introduced him to my friends. We found inspiration in the bars and cafes of Montmartre, liked to drink, and enjoyed the company of women. Hamid liked to watch me paint, particularly the nudes, telling me that sort of thing would never happen in Constantinople.'

Pierre went on to say that the models sometimes became his mistresses and they went out drinking together. 'He was amazed at how free they were after the constraints of the society he grew up in,' he added. 'He began to see some of them, buying them gifts as if he had money to throw around. Compared to some of us, he did.'

There was a look of shock on the faces in the room. Theodosia could see that some thought he was lying – an artist seeking attention.

'The first few days I was here, Hamid and I went out together and he showed me the famous sights of the city. Then he used to go out alone while I stayed in his house painting.'

'Do you know where he went?'

'I presumed it was to smoke hashish or opium, the latter being something he became addicted to in Paris – or to visit women. I could see that all this pressure was taking its toll on him. Then one day he came back with a huge grin on his face. When I asked him what the matter was, he declared he was in love. Knowing he loved women, I thought it wouldn't last, but I soon realised he meant it. Because I was his close confidant, he trusted me enough to tell me that this person was someone who his family would disapprove of, and the relationship was impossible because the family had already chosen someone for him. He wanted to convince them otherwise. I used to hear him arguing with his father, who often went to his room and berated him. Once, I heard something smash and a servant was sent to clean up a vase which was in pieces on the floor. He told me his father threw it at him in anger. I never really knew what took place, but most people in the household knew there was tension between them.'

The inspector looked across the room at Ferid Pasha, who did not blink an eye. It was no one's business what took place in his house – until now.

'Continue, monsieur.'

'Naturally, I laughed as at that point, I thought he was incapable of really falling in love. I was of the opinion it was lust.

'He assured me that this time it really was love. "As soon as I laid eyes on her, I was seized by a burning desire for her. I want her and no one else," he said. "She is a gift from Heaven; the light that rivals the sun. Compared to her, all other women are dull." That's when he told me he wanted to run away and marry her. Who is this woman, I asked?'

Pierre said he laughed even more when he heard he'd fallen for a woman who sold oranges outside the Grand Bazaar. '"You are not in Paris now," I said to him. "There you can live the Bohemian life; here you will ruin your family completely."'

By now the room was silent again. Everyone was on the edge of their seats, wide-eyed, hanging on to the artist's every word. Whatever was Hamid thinking of?

'Was this around the time he was arguing with his father?' Ibrahim asked.

'Yes. Hamid begged him to cancel the wedding, but the pasha said it would bring disgrace to the family and he had already done enough damage. "If you do not end this relationship now, I will send you to the far reaches of the empire," he told him.'

'For the purpose of this investigation, Monsieur Pierre, are you are telling us that Hamid begged his father to stop the marriage?'

'That is right.'

'Hmm, I see. Thank you. You may continue.'

'Eventually, his father won and Hamid was forced to conclude that he must go through with the marriage, but he would not stop seeing her.'

'By *her*, I presume you mean Gizem?'

'At the time I did not know her name. Knowing the marriage would go ahead, he asked if I would paint her portrait as he wanted to be reminded of her every day. It was to be my wedding present to him. Naturally, I agreed. That's when he started to take me with him. I met her the first time outside the Bayezid Gate.' Pierre paused and turned to face Gizem. 'And that's when I understood his feeling were genuine, because...' Pierre searched for the right words.

'Because?' the inspector asked, waiting patiently, his foot tapping on the carpet.

Pierre held his gaze. 'Because when I laid eyes on her, I also fell in love. It was not just her beauty which took my breath away. There was something about her that made me want to take her in my arms and never let her go. She hypnotized me just as she did Hamid.'

Tövbe! Shame! *Theos mou! Mon Dieu!* At this revelation there were exclamations in Turkish, Greek, and French; such was the surprise. 'The woman is a witch,' someone muttered. 'She has cast the evil eye on them.' Ayşe and Behice looked at each other in disbelief. Both had tears in their eyes. The pain and hurt Hamid had caused was beyond their wildest imagination.

Pierre told the inspector that, at first, he hid his feelings from Hamid, telling him that she was indeed someone special and he would be only too happy to paint her. It was decided that he would make sketches of her selling her oranges as the setting was full of character and, each night, Hamid would look at the sketches. When he was satisfied, he chose one but asked her to sit for Pierre in person to be sure he captured her features correctly. This took place in the room where she and Hamid made love. On these occasions, her friend at the market always looked out for her, enabling her to feel free to leave for a few hours at a time. At first Hamid stayed in the room watching the painting take shape, but after a while, he would wander to the hashish den, returning in time to escort her back. It was these comings and goings that Abdul Agha had witnessed and reported back to Theodosia, although he never saw what was taking place inside the room.

'Hamid bought her beautiful clothes for the portrait but she didn't want to wear them. Instead, she wore her simple kaftan with flowing sleeves, the neckline and sleeves delicately embroidered with shaded pink and gold tulips. I arranged her hair in a way that I thought suited the portrait, with a silk scarf tied around her hair in a band and her curls falling over one shoulder. Her beauty is such that she didn't need finery. As I started to paint her, I gained her confidence and we began to talk.

'The painting took a couple of weeks and each time she told me more about herself. The more I was with her, the more I wanted her for myself. I felt as if my chest would burst.'

'When did you tell Gizem Hanim about the good lady he was betrothed to?' Inspector Ibrahim asked.

Pierre thought about it for a moment. 'I knew I would lose a good friend by speaking out, yet at the same time, I loved her and didn't want to see her hurt, so it was just before the painting was finished. I purposely delayed completing it until a couple of days before the marriage.'

'How did Hamid take this? Did he think you had betrayed him?'

'Yes, he was furious. We had terrible arguments and Gizem was caught in the middle of it all. He said I was unfaithful: no longer a friend and that I should go back to Paris as soon as the painting was finished. One day the arguments were so bad he even pulled out a gun and threatened to shoot me until Gizem intervened. She was so upset that she told him she could never love a man with a temper like this. To make it worse, she stood next to me and said it had all been a grave mistake, and that it was me that she loved, not Hamid. At that point I thought he would kill us both. Thankfully, he stormed out of the room. Seeing Hamid's rage, I thought he was capable of anything and begged Gizem to come to Paris with me as I could take care of her. I even promised to become a Muslim for her and her father.'

At this point Inspector Ibrahim stood up and called for refreshments to be served as the heat was stifling and the atmosphere tense. He asked that no one leave the room, except to use the toilet and even then, they would be under police guard. During the ten minute break, no one spoke. They were all in a state of shock.

The refreshments over, the cross-examination began again.

'However, Monsieur Pierre, you did go to the wedding, did you not?'

'Hamid and I eventually decided that if I didn't, there would be too many questions asked by his family. If it all came out, it would have devastated them. For the time being, we put it behind us, even though we hardly spoke.'

'Hmm, I see. I put it to you then, that you did indeed have a motive to kill Hamid. In your eyes, he had hurt and deceived the woman you loved.'

Pierre shook his head despondently. 'I understood his frustration. He truly loved her, yet *I* was the one free to marry her. *I* was the one who could give her a good life – and she loved me. Yes, I did feel like killing him, but he was still my friend and I never could have brought myself to do such a thing. I am not capable of it.'

The inspector turned towards Gizem. 'Good lady, you have heard Monsieur Pierre's words. Is this true?'

Gizem's eyes looked from one to the other. 'Every single word, Efendim.' Then she began to sob.

The inspector allowed her time to compose herself. 'You said earlier that you lost your heart to Hamid. What changed?'

'My feelings for the Frenchman grew. I saw truth in his eyes. He is a gentle soul, a man who, like myself, had a hard life, and we shared a lot in common. I realised it was a fantasy to love Hamid, that's all. I was confused.'

'Are you confused now? Do you still love this man?'

Gizem looked at Pierre. 'I do, and despite them falling out, I know he would never hurt his friend.'

The inspector mulled over her words for a while and looked at his notes. 'I am putting this question to you both and I want a clear answer. Did you know if Behice Hanim was aware of Hamid's affair?'

Gizem said she didn't think so. Pierre, on the other hand, said he thought Behice suspected he had been seeing someone else.

'Why is that?' Ibrahim asked.

'Behice Hanim came to the room a few times to view the painting as Hamid had told her I was painting one for a wedding present. Gizem was never there. On these occasions, Behice was always accompanied by her maid, and the excuse for being there was that they had gone to look at fabrics in the Grand Bazaar. She approved of the painting and complimented me on my work.' There was a long pause in which the inspector sensed Pierre was holding something back.

'Go on, monsieur.'

'This was just before Hamid and I fell out. He was pleased she liked it and went out to get us coffee and sweets. It was on the last occasion that Behice found an unfinished poem he'd written for Gizem which he'd accidentally left lying on the table where I kept some of my paints. Unfortunately, her eyes fell upon it. "Oh," she said, her eyes lighting up as she started to read it, "my Hamid is a dark horse. He has written me a love letter." She began to read aloud the words:

> *"This is how I would die*
> *into the love I have for you:*
> *As pieces of cloud*
> *dissolve in sunlight."*

'It was another Rumi poem, which Behice recognised. She looked so happy. "I wonder when he was going to give me this?" she asked. I blushed with embarrassment. What could I say?

'She didn't stop there. "Maybe he has written more," she said. I was praying Hamid would come back soon before it got worse, but she was so excited, she opened a wooden box carved with his initials where he kept a few of his private possessions. She found two more and started to read them but quickly came to the realization that they were written by someone else.

'I could do nothing but look on in embarrassment, trying to divert her attention with small talk. She brushed me aside and I saw the look on her face drop. "These have been written by someone else. The handwriting is different." She called her maid over. "Allah have mercy on me. What is all this?" she cried out. "Are my eyes deceiving me?"

'Her maid looked equally shocked. "I fear not, my Hanimim," she replied. I stood there helpless. "Did you know about these?" Behice asked, waving the poems at me. In that moment I was stuck for words.'

Inspector Ibrahim asked Pierre what happened next.

'Hamid returned with our refreshments. As soon as he entered the room, he knew something bad had happened. Behice was holding the poems, tears rolling down her cheeks as her maid tried in vain to comfort her. "Behice, my darling one," Hamid said, but before he could say anything else, she threw the poems at him in anger, calling him the devil himself.

'Hamid was like a fish caught in a net, desperately trying to wriggle out of the mess he had created. He brushed it off, saying the ones he wrote were for her, the others were from some admirer and he'd meant to throw them away. Clearly, she didn't believe him and it only made things worse. Hamid asked me to go outside for a while until the situation was cleared up. As I walked down the stairs into the street, I could still hear their voices. I must have been outside for almost ten minutes when the ladies came out. They saw me on the opposite side of the road and Behice came over. "I'm so sorry you had to see that. I put you in a difficult position. It wasn't your fault."

'"Behice Hanim," I said, feeling deeply sorry for her, "I do hope you've sorted it out." She gave me a sweet smile. "Yes. You need not worry. Go back and finish the beautiful painting. I would be most disappointed not to receive it." I kissed the back of her hand and they left. Her maid quickly glanced back over her shoulder and gave me a sad look.

'I rushed back upstairs and found Hamid in an angry mood. When I asked if she believed him, he pointed to the shredded letters in the bin. The only ones he'd torn up were Gizem's. "I gave the other to her, assuring her it was written for her." He didn't want to talk about it anymore and told me we were going home. That night he got drunk and went out. I had no idea where he went but that's when I decided to tell him I'd fallen for his beloved.'

Theodosia watched with interest as Gizem and Behice listened to this with emotionless expressions. It seemed to her that Gizem was furious with Hamid for not telling her the truth. She thought that Behice too felt she had been deceived.

The inspector turned to Behice and asked her if Pierre's account was true. She nodded, commenting that she was very upset at what had taken place. He also asked Behice's maid if this was a true account of that day and she too agreed.

The inspector shook his head and added a few more notes in his folder. This was indeed a sorry state of affairs, which, like many cases he'd worked on, could have been prevented if only people behaved correctly. He glanced across at Pierre, who in that moment, looked around the room at the guests' icy glares, feeling as if he was in some way responsible, and was just about to continue speaking when Pierre's eyes settled on Behice, who was wiping away her eyes with her tears with her handkerchief.

'I am truly sorry, Behice Hanim,' Pierre said. 'If I could have prevented your pain, I would have done so. I was powerless.'

Behice ignored him, but by now everyone started whispering things to each other. It was truly a shocking moment and one that even Theodosia had not expected.

Abdul Agha sighed. 'Aman! Allah protect us,' he whispered to Theodosia. 'I knew all this spying would lead to trouble.'

She reminded him that all there were suffering at what had taken place. 'I agree, but the murderer sits here with us and still hasn't confessed. Let's not forget that.'

'I have another question, Monsieur Pierre,' Inspector Ibrahim said. 'You said earlier that Hamid was angry with you when you declared your love for Gizem. What did he do with that that gun?'

Pierre thought hard. 'I believe he put it back in the wooden box.'

'Why would he do that? Why not put it back in his jacket pocket?'

'I don't know. Sometimes he took his jacket off and lay it on the bed. That's usually when he put the gun in the box – for safe keeping.'

'Do you know if he had more than one gun?

'It's possible. A man in his position often possesses a few.'

The inspector showed the photograph of the gun which had been found during the search. 'Was it like this?'

Pierre looked surprised. 'That's it. I have a good memory and recalled the design of it when I first saw it. He said he bought it in Paris.'

'Did Behice Hanim and her maid see it on one of the days they were there?'

'It's likely.'

'Are you sure?'

'I'm almost sure because it was in the box when she found the poems.'

The inspector went over to Behice and her maid and asked them both to take a good look at it. 'Did you see Hamid's gun on that day?'

There was a moment's silence and Behice said yes, she had seen it. 'And you, Hanim Kizim?' Ibrahim said to the maid. She looked agitated and said yes too.

The inspector looked across at Selahattin, who noted that down. He turned back to Pierre. 'There is one more thing I would like to ask you, monsieur. If you love this lady as you say you do, why were you leaving Istanbul without her?'

'It's quite simple. I didn't have the money for two tickets, and besides, we weren't married. I promised to come back for her as soon as I could.'

Theodosia thought it was hard to read Inspector Ibrahim's face. Did he believe Pierre really would come back for Gizem?

'Thank you,' Ibrahim said. 'That will be all for the moment.' The inspector closed his file, took off his spectacles, and wiped his brow. The clock chimed three thirty and everyone was getting tired and irritable. Conducting an enquiry was never an easy task and each one presented its own problems. One had to tread carefully, let everyone know who was in control, and yet be sensitive enough to know when a person had more to say than he or she admitted to. Most of all, he enjoyed the psychology associated with a good investigation. It was a mind game. Who would break first?

CHAPTER 15

By now, it appeared that everyone in the room had come to realize Behice and Hamid's marriage was doomed from the start, but as yet no-one was any the wiser about who could have killed Hamid. The murderer still remained elusive. Even Theodosia wondered where all this questioning was leading. She also wondered if the last little investigation she'd undertaken with Abdul for the inspector had proved to be useful after all, or had they been on a wild goose chase.

'Where is all this leading?' asked Ferid Pasha. 'If you have any evidence, please show us. Our nerves are frayed enough and all this is making us worse.'

Ibrahim walked into the middle of the room again. All eyes were on him, wondering what he would say next. 'Patience, Efendim, patience. Something else that day made me curious. I wanted to know why Behice Hanim felt ill and excused herself to go and lie down. It seems that no one really understood why and she was there quite a long time. Even the doctor could not find anything seriously wrong with her.'

'The excitement of the day combined with the heat,' Hateme exclaimed. 'Many women experience all sorts of feelings from happiness to nausea on their wedding day. Throughout our life we grow up with the expectation of marriage and want it to be the best day of our lives: that and bearing healthy children. So it is hardly surprising she felt ill. Even we were nervous that everything should go well on the day. And then there was the vast amount of food served, extremely delicious and some of it quite rich.'

Most people in the room agreed with her, including the inspector. 'I agree whole heartedly with you, Hanimefendi. All the same, we would be neglectful in our duty if we didn't consider *why* she was ill. Being experienced in matters such as this, we could not rule out that the murderer intended to kill Behice as well, which is why we examined all the dishes just in case there were any traces of poison.'

Except for the police and palace officials, that had not occurred to most of those gathered there and they uttered loud gasps of disbelief. Who would try to kill such an innocent woman as Behice? Hafsa in particular, looked stricken. She tried to speak but the words would not come out.

He gave a little cough before his next statement. 'It came to my attention that two of the cooks that day once worked for in a certain household where someone died due to poisoning.'

Theodosia's heart missed a beat. She had a sinking feeling that he was going to make her talk about the incident with Zeynep and Maria, and that might affect her friendship with Hafsa, not to mention the reputation of both cooks.

Hateme and Ömer looked aghast. 'Who?' asked Hateme, annoyed at the inference that they employed unreliable people. 'We check out the people who work for us. Who are these cooks?'

Inspector Ibrahim looked at Theodosia and asked her to tell them about what took place when Maria was working with Zeynep. She had dreaded this moment.

'Maria once told me about an incident which took place when they were working together in the kitchen under a certain Master Yusuf, the pasha's chief cook.'

Hafsa looked confused. 'This is the first time I've heard of this. Why didn't you tell me before?'

'As no one was actually convicted, it didn't seem right to bring it up.' Theodosia recounted the story. 'You may have thought Zeynep had something to do with it and I did not want an injustice to occur by seeing her dismissed. After all, you told me you were happy with her, and I too, am happy with Maria; therefore, I thought it wise to let sleeping dogs lie.' Theodosia hoped Hafsa would understand. 'It was in one of my discussions with Inspector Ibrahim that the topic of murder by poisoning came up. I know from conversations with my late husband that such a thing is common. I certainly did not intend to rake up the past.' She felt conflicted about not telling Hafsa and hoped she would understand.

Before Hafsa could reply, the inspector continued. 'Knowing this story, we therefore had to rule out poisoning. Thankfully, we found nothing suspicious. Everything was fine and Hateme Hanim assured us they she and her chief cook keep a close eye on any poisons. The cooks, Zeynep and Maria, worked on the wonderful desserts together and I believe they worked in harmony. Both said this in their interviews. I do admit that some of the food was going off in the heat and that could have contributed to Behice's nausea. So, good people, you can rest assured that poison has been ruled out.'

Hafsa gave a deep sigh of relief. 'Mashallah! That at least is something, but I implore you, if you know who the murderer is, tell us, because I cannot take much more of this.'

At that moment there was a knock on the door and a policeman entered. He came straight over to Inspector Ibrahim and whispered in his ear. All eyes were on the pair as the inspector knitted his eyebrows together in a frown and nodded. He beckoned Selahattin Bey over and after the three had conferred in hushed tones, Ibrahim made an announcement.

'Ladies and gentlemen, something urgent has come up and I must conclude the discussion for the time being. I ask that you stay here until we resume. As it is stifling hot and you must be stiff with sitting in your chairs for so long, you may go onto the terrace and get some fresh air. Please do not wander around the grounds. My men will be noting your movements at all times. Refreshments will be served too. Hateme Hanim, please confer with your butler as to your requirements.' He looked at Ferid and Ömer. 'If you don't mind, I would like you both to accompany me.'

Everyone, startled, looked at one another, wondering what was going on but by now, the situation was unpredictable and both Ferid and Ömer told their wives not to worry. As they were heads of their families, it was only natural the inspector would want to involve them in whatever was taking place.

Theodosia whispered to Abdul, 'I have a feeling that this has something to do with our last investigation. Let's hope it has been successful.'

The guests, resigned by now to the situation, filed out onto the terrace where a soft breeze cooled the summer heat. Some took a walk to the water's edge while others stretched their legs and then settled down to rest and partake in light refreshments and bite-sized *böreks* and sweets. Not even the sweet trilling of songbirds in their decorative wooden and iron cages that stood on specially made tables or hung from chains in the ceiling could lighten their mood. The day's revelations had turned their world upside down and few had little appetite for food.

Theodosia took a walk with Abdul to discuss things in private and then returned to the terrace, where she seated herself next to Katerina and the Grand Duchess Irena, who had been shunned by both Hateme and Hafsa.

'Don't judge me too harshly,' Irena said, dismally.

Katerina and Theodosia looked at her with sadness. She was despondent now, but they knew an incident like this, no matter how bad it was, wouldn't stop her having affairs in the future. 'We've been friends a long time. Who are we to judge?' Katerina replied.

Theodosia squeezed her hand. 'Having an affair is not the same as committing a murder.' She wanted to add that in her opinion, the Grand Duchess had shown poor judgment but she kept silent.

The guests sat around in small groups, seeking out the ones they thought they trusted the most. Gizem sat with her father and Pierre at one end of the terrace. No one wanted to even speak with them. She covered her shoulders with her shawl, as if trying to hide herself from the judgmental looks of Hafsa and Hateme. Pierre put his arm around her and whispered soothing words in her ear.

'Allah help us,' Hateme said to Hafsa, when she saw this. 'What a disgrace. We will be the laughing stock of all Istanbul.'

'Look!' someone shouted out. 'The boat is leaving the mooring dock. 'The inspector is on it with Ferid and Ömer Efendi, and the palace officials.'

Everyone – except Gizem, her father, and Pierre – rushed to the far side of the terrace near the water's edge to take a look. Selahattin and two policemen stayed behind.

'What's going on?' Hafsa and Hateme cried out. 'Where are they going?'

They watched the boat weave its way between the ships, ferries, and smaller vessels until it looked like a small speck when it reached the other side of the Bosphorus, before returning back to their seats more confused than ever. Hateme and Hafsa tried to leave the terrace but were met by Selahattin, who urged them to go back. Both women were at their wit's end, cursing Gizem for their woes. Hateme gave a loud, exasperated sigh and they reluctantly went back to the terrace. Selahattin Bey was like Inspector Ibrahim in that he abhorred the way some of the privileged classes looked down on others as if they were the cause of all evils. However, he had learned that putting on a pleasant smile in the line of duty was far more helpful to the situation in hand.

Outside, the others asked if they'd found anything out. 'They continue to keep us in the dark,' Hateme replied. She went to sit alone, basking in her deep disappointment in her husband and son. Hafsa went to comfort Ayşe and Behice, who were no longer speaking with each other after the revelations. Like everyone else, they were exhausted.

It was three hours before the boat returned. By this time, the warmth of the day had eased and a cool sea breeze blew from the north, carrying with it the invigorating scent of the salty sea air combined with the fragrance of flowers from the Garden of Enchantment and the resin of pine trees from the surrounding landscape. The men alighted; they included Inspector Ibrahim, who was carrying a portmanteau, several more policemen, and the same palace officials. Theodosia noticed another man with them – a small, stocky man in a suit and wearing a fez. Theodosia also saw that Ferid had returned but not Ömer.

Where's Ömer?' she said to Abdul. 'This doesn't look good at all.' He agreed.

Selahattin Bey greeted the men and both he and the inspector remained in deep discussions for a while before the group walked back towards the house. Out on the terrace, the group prepared themselves for more distressing news. Selahattin Bey was the one to call them all back in the room. 'Please go back to your seats,' he said matter-of-factly. 'Inspector Ibrahim will be with you in a moment.'

Five minutes later, Ibrahim entered the room with the palace officials, who resumed their seats and prepared to take notes again. This time two more policemen entered the room and stood by the door, with their hands clasped behind their back. Selahattin was carrying the inspector's portmanteau and stood next to it near the palace officials as if guarding it with his life. Ferid did not enter the room with them.

'Where's my husband?' Hateme asked, anxiously. Hafsa asked the same question.

At that moment, Theodosia noticed that the inspector looked as though he was carrying the weight of the world on his shoulders. She had seen the same look on Alexander's face when he was about to close a trial. 'They are both helping us with our enquiries,' he replied. 'For the moment, we will continue without them.'

Hafsa demanded to see Ömer, but the inspector urged her to sit down. Katerina put her hand on her shoulder to comfort her, saying that there must be a good reason and she must not worry. That was easier said than done. The look on the inspector's face told them the time was near: the murderer was about to be uncovered. The tense atmosphere was once again filled with expectation.

The inspector gave a little cough to clear his throat. 'I am sorry that I had to leave you in a state of distress for so long. Information came to light which urgently needed our attention.' Ibrahim looked at Pierre. 'Monsieur Maurin, let us recapitulate if I may. You said that Hamid often kept his revolver in the room where you painted?'

'That's correct,'

'So the last person to see the gun was yourself and the deceased?'

'I cannot tell you if anyone else saw it after he took the painting away. We were not exactly close at that point.'

'For the purpose of this interview, I am showing you a photo of

Hamid's gun again.' He came towards him and held it closer. 'You are sure this is the one.'

He walked around the room giving everyone time to look at it again. He stopped in front of Behice. 'And you, too, are certain, Behice Hanim?'

'Absolutely'

'And your maid?' He showed it to her too.

'Quite sure.'

Seeing her daughter and the maid trembling with fear, Hafsa interrupted. 'Please, Inspector, my daughter has suffered enough. Get to the point.'

The inspector gestured to Selahattin to bring over the bag. He opened it and took out a brown linen cloth and in front of everyone carefully unwrapped it to show a gun which he held between his finger and thump at the end of the nozzle. Everyone gasped aloud.

'What about this gun? Have any of you ever seen it before?' Again he walked around the room showing it to everyone. Some reeled back in horror, frowns and confusion on their faces.

'What about you, Monsieur Pierre?'

Pierre looked closely. 'It's remarkably similar to Hamid's. Very similar, except...'

'Except what?'

'It doesn't have the star and crescent on it. It has similar elegant scrollwork but the ivory grip looks a little different. It has more texture, a little more worn.'

The inspector thanked him. 'Indeed, Monsieur Maurin, you have the keen eye of an artist.' He walked back into the centre of the room.

'As you see, it's a similar Velo-Dog.' He paused. 'Has anyone in this room seen it before?' The silence was unbearable as his eyes scanned the faces. 'Rest assured that no one is beyond the law, so I am asking you once more because it belongs to someone in this room.'

Hateme put her hand on her chest, as if the pain was unbearable. Without Ferid, she seemed vulnerable.

The inspector sighed. 'Alright: I *had* hoped that the perpetrator would find God and own up, but it appears not. He gave a nod to the policemen, who went outside and brought in the stranger who had been on the boat with him. The man took off his fez and bowed. Seeing the looks on everyone's faces, he too seemed apprehensive.

'Allow me to introduce Ahmet Bey,' Ibrahim said. The man bowed again, this time a little lower, as everyone stared at him with great curiosity.

'Ahmet Bey is from Galata. He has a small business dealing in firearms. If you would, Beyefendi, please point out the person who you gave this gun to.'

Theodosia could not recall a time before when she'd been in a room filled with so much mental and emotional strain.

The man slowly lifted his arm and pointed to Behice's maid. 'That's her,' he said. He knew his words were of vital importance and his voice was shaking with fear.

An audible gasp went around the room. Everyone's eyes fixed on the maid, whose face was as white as a sheet. Tears rolled down her face when she saw the way everyone looked at her. 'It wasn't my fault,' she shouted out. 'In the name of Allah, please believe me. I only...'

Hafsa jumped up from her seat, her eyes glaring with anger. 'You

– of all people. A person we trusted, how…'

Inspector Ibrahim stopped her. 'Hanimefendi! Please sit down. I have not finished.'

Ahmet Bey looked terrified, as if he himself was responsible for killing Hamid. The inspector waved his hand at him, beckoning him to stay calm. 'Continue please.'

'A… a young lady came to see me about two weeks ago and asked if I had any small guns. When I asked what type, at first she said she didn't know, but it had to be one that she could hide in her purse. That's when I showed her a few in a catalogue. She chose the one there.' He gestured to the one lying on the cloth on the table.

Ahmet Bey was illegally dealing in firearms, and as he was wary of getting caught he told her he could only sell her one on the proviso she didn't say where she got it.

'The lady seemed pleased and agreed to take it. I told her that I would have it the next day. She was fine with that and even offered to pay more than I quoted if there was no record of the sale. Naturally that suited me. I asked what her name was and she gave me her calling card, telling me that her maid would pick it up. If anyone asked, I was not to mention our meeting. She left and I arranged to get the gun for her.' The palace officials intermittently looked up at him as they made their notes, their pens flying across the page, making sure they got every word down.

'Inspector Ibrahim Bey, I have sold to men and women alike, but this lady – well, she was exceptionally well-dressed and I wondered why she didn't go to a licensed dealer. Why come to me?'

Ahmet hesitated. 'May I assure you,' Inspector Ibrahim said, 'that

I promised you that you would not be charged for illegal trading if you spoke the truth, so please continue and tell us what happened the next day.'

'I half-expected no one to come, but just as I was about to close, that lady came.' He pointed to the maid again. 'Her words were, "You have something for me to pick up." I showed her the calling card. "Yes," she said. "Is it ready?" I prepared the gun with a small box of ammunition, wrapped it up, and gave it to her. She handed me the money, which I counted in front of her. Then she asked for the calling card as she wanted to remain anonymous. I gave it to her. She thanked me and left.

'Curiosity made me go to the door and look to see which way she headed. At that time of night, the area is still quite busy with seamen and itinerant vendors, and I noticed her head along the seafront in a northerly direction. Then she disappeared in the throng of people coming and going to the taverns and bars. As I turned to go inside, that's when I saw she had dropped the calling card. I picked it up and thought no more about it until... until someone called by making enquiries.'

Inspector Ibrahim reached into the inside pocket of his jacket. 'Just to be clear, is this the calling card?'

The man looked and it nodded.

Everyone hung on to their words. Ibrahim looked at the cream coloured card. 'Behice Hanim, I believe this belongs to you.' He handed it to her.

Theodosia was having a hard time taking all this in. She was sure her heart would burst in her chest at any moment. She looked at

Hafsa, who was as white as a ghost, and felt pity for her, knowing how sensitive she was. Surely it couldn't be what they thought?

'Behice, my darling,' Hafsa said, the words sticking in her throat. 'Please tell me there's a mistake. It's too far-fetched.' Hafsa shook her daughter's arm. 'Speak, child. Tell me this isn't true.'

Behice's face appeared cold and unsympathetic and her ears deaf to the groans and distress around her.

Inspector Ibrahim stood in front of her and said calmly, 'Behice Hanim, this gun was found hidden in your room. I am arresting you for the murder of your husband, Hamid, on the day of... your wedding. Your maid is also charged as an accomplice.' He beckoned the two policemen over to take them away immediately.

Hafsa, overcome with grief, fainted. The inspector's words were so overwhelming it was hard for everyone, including Theodosia, to take in. So dumfounded were they that at first no one was able to speak. Hateme held the flat of her hands to her temple in disbelief. 'Behice of all people – the woman we all loved. You took my son away from me. May Allah have pity on your soul.'

When Behice rose from her seat, Theodosia was amazed that she showed no sign of emotion; just the icy glare she'd maintained throughout the day. It was as if she had detached herself from the scene; that someone else had committed the crime, not her. Theodosia recalled Alexander's stories of both men and women he had worked with and how easily they were able to disassociate themselves from reality.

As the two women were being led out of the room, the maid broke free and before anyone had time to stop her, rushed to a side table where there were still trays of food, picked up a knife, and stabbed herself in the chest, falling next to Katerina, who let out a terrified scream. *'Theos mou!'* she said instinctively in Greek. 'My God! Someone save her.'

Two policemen hastily grabbed her, pulled out the knife, and snatched a napkin from the table to stem the bleeding. She was carried out of the room unconscious, leaving a spreading wet patch of blood on the exquisite carpet. The maid's action had so appalled them that suddenly everyone started to speak at once.

The inspector called for calm. 'This is not the outcome any of us had hoped for, but it is indeed true. It took us a while, but we now have irrefutable proof of who was behind Hamid's murder. Tests on the gun, which was found hidden in her room, will conclusively prove that Behice Hanim is the murderer. Further interviews will be conducted at police headquarters in the city.

'I thank you for your patience and pray that you will all find peace soon. I may need to speak with some of you again, but for now, you are free to go. Allah be with you and keep you safe.'

People slowly started to file out of the room, mumbling words of shock and dabbing their eyes. Outside in the reception hall, a policeman stood next to Ferid, who had not been allowed in the room for fear he would show his emotions and give something away, approached his wife and held her tightly, tears streaking both their cheeks. The inspector offered them his condolences. No words could ease their sorrow. Then Ferid was asked to accompany the police back to the waiting barge with them. In the meantime, Hafsa had been told that her husband was already at the police station helping them with the enquiry.

After the police barge left, the other guests were allowed to leave. Hafsa was too distressed to walk alone and both Katerina and the Grand Duchess helped her to the barge. A heartbroken Ayşe followed behind them, her shoulders shaking with her silent tears.

Theodosia and Abdul Agha were among the last.

The inspector came to speak with Theodosia. 'If it's alright with you, after I have finalized this case, I would like to pay you a visit.'

'Certainly.' They shook hands and stepped into the boat.

Darkness was now descending on the city and as they rode across the water, she stared at the lights of Ferid and Hateme's yali with sadness. 'Aman,' she sighed, and made the sign of the cross.

Abdul looked at her with sorrow. He had no need to ask what she was thinking.

CHAPTER 16

THEODOSIA WOKE FROM a deep sleep, stretched out, and lay for a long time in bed, mulling over the previous day's events. She saw that curtains had been opened and a tray of food was on her bedside table. There was a soft knock on the bedroom door. It was Calliope, who came to check on her.

'You were fast asleep when I came earlier and I brought your breakfast here as I didn't want to wake you up.' She stood at the end of the bed. 'Do you need anything else; maybe another pot of hot tea or coffee?'

'No thank you, Calliope: orange juice is fine.' She pulled herself up and propped her head against the soft pillows. 'I was so tired, I barely remembered coming to bed.'

'How did it go? I just saw Abdul outside but he wouldn't say anything. Did the inspector find the murderer?'

Theodosia patted the bed for Calliope to sit next to her. 'It was one of the worst days of my life. You'll never believe who the killer was?' Calliope braced herself. 'Behice!'

Calliope reached for the small cross she wore around her neck and kissed it. 'Aman! May the blessed Virgin save her: that soft, beautiful woman – her father's little angel. I can't believe it.'

'Sin is everywhere,' Theodosia replied with a deep sigh. 'Even angels sin.'

There was a long silence and seeing that Theodosia was still trying to come to terms with it, Calliope suggested she stay in bed for the rest of the day. 'Electra has German lessons in Pera. I can take care of everything. Get some sleep. You'll feel much better.'

'What would I do without you?' Theodosia squeezed her hand. 'Thank you, but I can't spend all day in bed – and neither can I forget what has just happened. Too many innocent people are now suffering.'

'As you wish. At least let me lay out your clothes.'

'Find something cheerful, please.'

Calliope looked in Theodosia's extensive wardrobe and pulled out a satin cream day dress with pink and red roses in ribbon-work on the bodice. 'How about this? It's perfect for a summer's day.' She laid it out for her and left the room.

It was another hour before Theodosia finally left her room and Calliope was in the hallway with Maria. 'Kyria Theodosia, Calliope has just told me about Behice. I am in shock.'

'We all are, Maria, but what's done cannot be undone.' She headed to the drawing room, saying she didn't want to be disturbed.

The sound of birds chirping in the bushes filled the room when she opened the window. Looking at the garden and the view of the boats on the blue water, Theodosia could have been forgiven for thinking it had all been a bad dream, but the open diary on her desk alongside one of Alexander's notebooks, reminded her it was real. She sat at the desk and flicked through the things she'd written over the past few weeks. There in front of her were her words of excitement and joy at receiving the wedding invitation, but the more she turned the pages, the more she saw how her words described the descent into the unknown, her anguish for her friends, and her intense desire for Alexander to envelope her in love and guide her from the grave. When he gave her the diary, never in her wildest dreams had she expected it to be filled with such dark thoughts, yet there it all was, neat and tidy with her fine calligrapher's pen in deep indigo ink.

She had been too exhausted to write last night, afraid that in such a state she might spill ink on the page and ruin it, so she'd purposely left it until today when her mind was clearer. She picked up the pen, dipped it in the inkpot, and prepared to write, but her hand started to shake. How could she write what took place? She put the pen down and paced the room, reminding herself that life must go on. After another ten minutes, she sat down to write again. *My beloved Alexander, yesterday was not a good day. In fact, I am so shaken by recent events, I can barely write at all except to say that I feel your arms around me always. My head is still in darkness and my hand will not let me write what is on my mind. For the moment, I will amuse myself with the tranquility of the garden and the cheerful sound of songbirds. Yours, Theodosia.*

She blotted the page, closed the book, and stared at the blue sky, watching the clouds floating effortlessly by. To cheer her up, she picked up the latest fashion magazines and went outside on to the terrace. Half-heartedly, she flicked through copies of *Vogue*, *The Delineator*, *The Designer*, and *La Nouvelle Mode*, but her thoughts kept returning to the moment Behice was accused and her poor maid attempting to kill herself. She wondered how long it would be until the nasty business appeared in the newspapers.

It was two days later when Inspector Ibrahim called to see her – two long days that seemed like an eternity. Calliope showed him into the drawing room and Theodosia asked that they not be disturbed.

'Well, Inspector, I have not been able to sleep without taking a draught, such has been my distress.'

'I came as soon as everything was finalized. Behice's fingerprints proved she pulled the trigger and she's made a written confession. Her maid, poor woman, is recovering in the hospital under police guard.'

He began to tell her what happened after they left the yali on the day of the gathering, and the events leading up to it.

'I must confess that for a while I was beginning to think the murder would be inconclusive as everyone seemed to have an alibi. It's thanks to your suggestion that I checked Ahmet Bey because of Alexander's prior dealings with him – that's what really produced the outcome. We were already aware he operated his illegal firearms activities from Galata and kept a close eye on him, but he is a wily and cautious man: always one step ahead of the police. Considering the people involved in this sorry story, it never occurred to me that any one of them would go to such a person. All had the means to purchase pistols and pay a little baksheesh to keep it quiet in order for it not to show up in the records. You'd be surprised how often it happens.'

The inspector went on to say that he began to suspect Behice was not as innocent as she claimed due to her apparent faked illness, but until the gun was found he had no evidence.

'Behice knew Ferid Pasha's house well, and more importantly, where Hamid's room was. She asked him to meet her in that room. It was a set-up, and he didn't realise. It appears that she told him she had a special gift for him which she wanted to give him in private because she'd quarrelled with him after finding the poems. She wanted to put the episode behind her and he agreed. That's when she suggested she give it to him in his room.'

'Did he know she'd faked her illness?' Theodosia asked.

'I doubt it because he went to his room before her.'

'So she wanted to make sure people thought she was lying down in another room when the shooting occurred?'

'It seems that way. Her maid confirmed she was unwell at the time.'

Theodosia could envisage it – the maid, sneaking about in the upstairs hallway to make sure no one else was around when her mistress entered Hamid's room. 'So the maid saw the murder take place?'

'No. She heard it. She was keeping an eye out for Behice. After the shots were fired, Behice rushed back to lie on the bed, handing the gun back to the maid for safe-keeping.'

'Are you saying that the maid had the gun on her throughout the marriage ceremony?'

'That's right. She confessed as much when she came round. We examined the purse used on that day and the pistol fitted into it quite nicely. No one would have detected there was more than a comb and a few personal items in it.'

The pair was silent for a few moments. 'I also suspected the gentle Behice was not as soft as she appeared after Pierre told me of her fiery temper that day. She fooled us all with her innocent ways.'

'She certainly did,' replied Theodosia. 'But tell me, what happened when you went to see Ahmet Bey?'

'At first he denied selling such a gun, saying he only had the catalogues, but after I threatened him, saying he would go to prison if he didn't co-operate, his tongue loosened. I then assured him I would go easy on him if he told the truth. Reluctantly he agreed. I showed him a picture of Behice from one of the society magazines and he recognised her straight away. "She was the one who bought the gun; the maid just picked it up," he said. I left saying that if he could recall anything else, I would be grateful.

'He later recalled the calling card at Ferid Pasha's yali. That's when I concluded the meeting while we went to search Ömer Pasha's household. As it was at the pasha's house, I wanted him there. I also asked Ferid Pasha in order that he understood the gravity of the situation and could see there was no mistake. When we left you, we went straight to the house where several of my investigators and Ahmet Bey were waiting, and searched it from top to bottom. The gun was found wrapped in a silk cloth in one of Behice's jewellery boxes. After it was discovered, we returned to conclude the meeting.'

'All except Ömer Pasha?'

'He was in such a state that we could not risk him telling anyone what had happened, so it was decided to take him to the police station. It was for this same reason that we kept Ferid Pasha out of the room at the last moment.'

Inspector Ibrahim shook his head despondently. 'Behice confessed to killing Hamid because she realized he had fallen for the woman in the painting and wanted revenge. When questioned about involving the maid, she declared coldly, "She was willing to do anything for me. I never would have been caught if she hadn't been so clumsy and dropped my calling card." She did not even ask after her health after she'd stabbed herself.'

Theodosia was appalled at the girl's lack of care for her maid, who had risked everything for her. 'So she almost got away with it,' Theodosia said.

'Almost.'

Ibrahim thanked her for remembering that Alexander had written about the gun dealer in one of his notebooks and appreciated the effort she put into locating his notes. 'We really have to thank him too, you know. If he hadn't been so meticulous with his cases... well, who knows what would the outcome would have been. It's likely that Behice might have got away with it.'

'What will happen to her?' Theodosia asked.

'The sultan has taken a personal interest in this case. He was kept updated by his officials, and has asked that we keep the matter low key. He asked for a meeting yesterday evening with the Grand Imam and myself, and has concluded that it was a crime of passion. The imam wants to see justice served, so after much discussion, it was decided that she should be exiled to a place near Bodrum. There she will remain until the sultan sees fit to bring her back to Constantinople. When the maid recovers, she will be transferred to a prison for three years.'

Theodosia gave a little half-smile. 'So Behice will live a comfortable life in exile while the poor maid suffers the harshness of life in prison.' It was a statement rather than a question.

'As you are well aware, justice is not equal.'

Theodosia walked him outside where his carriage was waiting. 'What about Pierre and the orange seller – Gizem?'

'That, my dear Theodosia, is one of the good parts of this story. Gizem's father allowed her to marry him, and Ferid Pasha and Hateme Hanim apologized for their anger towards them. In a gesture of reconciliation, they gave them money to go to France. They leave at the weekend.'

'Well, at least something positive came from this. Pierre and Gizem are united now.'

Calliope waited until the inspector had left and brought a glass of rose sherbet out to her.

'Put it there,' Theodosia said, gesturing to the table on the terrace. 'I must do something first.'

She went into the garden, where Abdul Agha was planting a new bush. He waited for her to say something. She told him what had transpired and thanked him for his help.

He put his hand on his heart. 'I was here for monsieur, now I am here for you, Madame Theodosia.'

That evening, Katerina called round. 'I feel sorry for the maid. Who would have suspected Behice of being so cold and calculating?'

'I agree.' Theodosia inhaled deeply. 'But love, dear Katerina, can be a blessing and also a curse.'

'How right you are. Anyway, now that is all over, I've brought you something.'

Theodosia looked surprised. 'What is it?'

'Close your eyes. Go on, no peeping, and hold out your hand.'

Theodosia did as she was told and felt Katerina place something in the palm of her hand. 'Now you can open them.'

'What on earth is this?' Theodosia asked, her eyes widening.

'Three tickets to Paris. You, Electra, and I, are going for a week's holiday. It's all arranged. We leave on the Orient Express next week. There's something else too.'

'This generosity is too much,' Theodosia replied. A smile crossed her face: the first real smile in a few weeks. 'What's the other thing? Tell me. Surely it cannot surpass this.'

Katerina went outside the room and asked Calliope to call Electra.

When Electra entered the room, she gave Katerina a peck on the cheek. 'I see by the look on Mama's face that already your presence has enlivened the house.'

Katerina was anxious to complete her surprise. 'Go on, dear child; give your mother the good news.'

'Mama, Signore Salvatini has entered me in a piano competition in Paris. He says I am ready to make my debut.'

Theodosia was speechless for a moment or two and then gave her daughter a big hug. 'Oh, my precious one, I am so proud of you, but why did you not tell me before?'

'Because you were too absorbed in Hamid's murder and so I

purposely waited until it was over.'

'Well, what can I say? I am lost for words. This is certainly the most wonderful gift and just the tonic I needed. Bless you.' She wiped away a tear, but this time it was a tear of happiness, not sadness.

That evening, Theodosia felt as if the dark cloud had left her and she opened her diary at the last entry. She wanted to tell Alexander what the inspector had said but instead found herself writing something quite different. This time her hand was steady and in her best handwriting she began:

My darling Alexander, the light that guides me always. Today the darkness that has absorbed me for the past few weeks has left me. I had good news. Our precious daughter has excelled in her piano lessons and will be competing in Paris. Katerina and I will be going with her and spending a week there. I wish you were here to see her perform, but I know she will perform well, as your soul will be with her on stage to guide her.

I kiss your goodness,

Your loving Theodosia.

She blotted the words and then read them aloud. As she did, she heard the patter of raindrops on the window. What a relief! The summer heat was suddenly cooled by an unexpected downpour. 'Kismet,' she said to herself with a smile while opening the window to feel the raindrops on her hand. The heavens opened, cleansing her heart and wiping away the sorrows of Hamid's murder. It was time to move on.

ALSO BY THE AUTHOR

The Asia Minor Trilogy

The Embroiderer

The Carpet Weaver of Uşak

Seraphina's Song

*

WWII

Midnight in Istanbul

In the Shadow of the Pyrenees

The Song of the Partisans

The Viennese Dressmaker

The Secret of the Grand Hôtel du Lac

The Poseidon Network

Conspiracy of Lies

The Blue Dolphin

Code Name Camille (Novella)

*

Colours of Aegean Dreams: A Greek Odyssey
– A Colouring Book for Adults

Website:

www.kathryngauci.com

To sign up to my newsletter,
please visit my website and fill out the form.

AUTHOR BIOGRAPHY

Kathryn Gauci is a critically acclaimed international, bestselling, author who produces strong, colourful, characters and riveting storylines. She is the recipient of numerous major international awards for her works of historical fiction.

Kathryn was born in Leicestershire, England, and studied textile design at Loughborough College of Art and later at Kidderminster College of Art and Design where she specialised in carpet design and technology. After graduating, she spent a year in Vienna, Austria, before moving to Greece to work as carpet designer in Athens for six years. There followed another brief period in New Zealand before eventually settling in Melbourne, Australia.

Before turning to writing full-time, Kathryn ran her own textile design studio in Melbourne for over fifteen years, work which she enjoyed tremendously as it allowed her the luxury of travelling worldwide, often taking her off the beaten track and exploring other cultures. *The Embroiderer* is her first novel; a culmination of those wonderful years of design and travel, and especially of those glorious years in her youth living and working in Greece. It has since been followed by more novels set in both Greece and Turkey. *Seraphina's Song, The Carpet Weaver of Uşak, The Poseidon Network, The Blue Dolphin: A WWII Novel,* and *Midnight in Istanbul: A WWII Espionage Thriller*

Code Name Camille, written as part of *The Darkest Hour*

Anthology: WWII Tales of Resistance, became a **USA TODAY** Bestseller in the first week of publication.

The Secret of the Grand Hôtel du Lac became an Amazon Best Seller in both German Literature and French Literature.

Both ***The Secret of the Grand Hôtel du Lac*** and ***The Blue Dolphin*** received **The Hemingway Finalist Award 2021 (CIBA) 20th Century Wartime Fiction**

The Poseidon Network received The Hemingway Award 2020 – 1st Place Best in Category – Chanticleer International Book Awards (CIBA) 20th Century Wartime Fiction.

The Viennese Dressmaker *received* The Hemingway Award 2022 – 1st Place Best in Category – Chanticleer International Book Awards (CIBA) 20th Century Wartime Fiction and The Coffee Pot Book Club Book of the Year Award - Gold Medal 2022 - 20th Century Historical Fiction

In the Shadow of the Pyrenees received The Hemingway Award 2023 – 1st Place Best in Category – Chanticleer International Book Awards (CIBA) 20th Century Wartime Fiction, The Coffee Pot Book Club Book of the Year Award - Gold Medal 2023 – 20th Century Historical Fiction, and Readers Favourite Gold Medal 2024 – Fiction- Historical – Event/Era.

The Song of the Partisans received the Readers' Favourite 2023 Gold Medal Award for Military Fiction.